TREASURY OF CHILDREN'S
POETRY

TREASURY OF CHILDREN'S POETRY

EDITED BY ALISON SAGE
FOREWORD BY MICHAEL ROSEN

HUTCHINSON

LONDON SYDNEY AUCKLAND JOHANNESBURG

Contents

Foreword by Michael Rosen 8

Foreword

In this Treasury of Poetry you will find a host of people who have looked for very special ways of talking to you. That's what poetry is: special, odd, fascinating, intriguing, peculiar, thrilling, musical ways of talking. Poets are people who spend a good deal of time trying to mix and move the thoughts they have and the words they know until it sounds right, feels good and says what they want to say. And the dazzling and amazing thing about all this is that there never is just one or even two or three ways to do this. When you turn the pages of this book, you'll keep coming across new thoughts, new ways of writing, new sounds, new rhythms.

Listen to Grace Nichols – she tells us what she thinks about the sea at exactly the same time as she tells us what the sea *sounds* like:

> "sea timeless
> sea timeless
> sea timeless"

Or Percy Bysshe Shelley, nearly two hundred years ago, tells us a story about a great king called Ozymandias. He was a "king of kings", Shelley tells us, but hundreds of years later not very much of his statue remains. Shelley brings together pictures, as if we were flicking through photos: a great king, a desert, a broken statue. We are left to figure out what this feels like, what it all means. By bringing the pictures together in one poem, he enables us to see them contrasting with each other, as if one was a comment on the other.

And then turn back to those weird things we call nursery rhymes. What a crazy bit of film it would be to see a cat playing a fiddle, a cow jumping over the moon, a little dog laughing and a dish running away with a spoon. But if it was just told in pictures it would be missing something: all that rhythm and those perfect rhymes: "diddle" and "fiddle", "moon" and "spoon". Listen to the first letters of "cat" and "cow", "little" and "laughed", "see" and "such" – it's as if the music from the cat's fiddle is playing a dance, and the sound and rhythms of the words bump and bounce us along. A crazy bit of music and film all done with thirty words. Isn't that magic?

You can find all kinds of magic here: sometimes strange characters speak, like Lewis Carroll's walrus and carpenter; sometimes poets talk straight at us and say things like: "I like the town on rainy nights" or "I guess the country can be nice" or "I should like to rise and go, where the golden apples grow". Something as ordinary as rain might suddenly seem different and strange, because in Spike Milligan's words it comes through "holes in the sky".

And in "Full Fathom Five", William Shakespeare conjures up a picture of a skeleton in the sea turning to coral and pearls – beauty and horror combined. He says that it suffers a "sea-change". A "sea-change"? You might be watching television one day and you might hear someone say that the weather or a football team has gone through a "sea-change" and that person might not know that those words came from someone writing four hundred years ago, someone who did such wonderful things with words that people all over the world repeat what he once wrote about change without even knowing it.

Poetry can change the world we see into something new. And once you know *that*, you need never think again that the world has to be the way it is now. That's magic. That's poetry.

MICHAEL ROSEN

PART ONE

Nursery Rhymes and First Poems

Peter, Peter, Pumpkin-Eater

P ETER, Peter, pumpkin-eater;
Had a wife and couldn't keep her;
He put her in a pumpkin shell,
And there he kept her very well.

Peter, Peter, pumpkin-eater;
Had another and didn't love her;
Peter learned to read and spell,
And then he loved her very well.

Jack Be Nimble

J ACK be nimble, Jack be quick,
And Jack jump over the candlestick.

JESSIE WILLCOX SMITH

13

Tom, Tom, the Piper's Son

Tom, Tom, the piper's son,
Stole a pig and away did run;
The pig was eat, and Tom was beat,
And Tom ran crying down the street.

Humpty Dumpty

Humpty Dumpty
Sat on the wall,
Humpty Dumpty
Had a great fall.
All the king's horses
And all the king's men
Couldn't put Humpty
Together again.

Jack and Jill

JACK and Jill went up the hill,
  To fetch a pail of water;
Jack fell down and broke his crown,
And Jill came tumbling after.

Up Jack got and home did trot,
As fast as he could caper;
He went to bed to mend his head,
With vinegar and brown paper.

Hey Diddle Diddle

Hey diddle diddle, the cat and the fiddle,
The cow jumped over the moon;
The little dog laughed
To see such fun,
And the dish ran away with the spoon.

Mary, Mary, Quite Contrary

Mary, Mary, quite contrary,
How does your garden grow?
With silver bells and cockle shells
And pretty maids all in a row.

Baa, Baa, Black Sheep

Baa, baa, black sheep,
Have you any wool?
Yes sir, yes sir
Three bags full;
One for the master,
And one for the dame,
And one for the little boy
Who lives down the lane.

Polly Put the Kettle On

POLLY put the kettle on,
Susy took it off;
Aunt Jemima's little girl,
Has got the whooping cough.

Ring-a-ring-a-roses

RING-a-ring-a-roses
A pocket full of posies.
Atishoo! Atishoo!
We all fall down.

See-Saw, Margery Daw

SEE-saw, Margery Daw,
Johnny shall have a new master;
Johnny shall have but a penny a day,
Because he can't go any faster.

Little Miss Muffet

LITTLE Miss Muffet
Sat on a tuffet,
Eating her curds and whey;
Along came a spider,
And sat down beside her,
And frightened Miss Muffet away.

I Love Little Pussy

I love little pussy, her coat is so warm,
And if I don't hurt her she'll do me no harm.
So I won't pull her tail, nor drive her away,
But pussy and I together will play.

One, Two, Three, Four, Five

O NE, two, three, four, five,
Once I caught a fish alive.
Six, seven, eight, nine, ten,
Then I put it back again.
"Why did you let it go?"
"Because it bit my finger so."
"Which finger did it bite?"
"This little finger on my right."

One for a Tangle

ONE for a tangle,
One for a curl,
One for a boy,
One for a girl,
One to make a parting,
One to tie a bow,
One to blow the cobwebs out
And one to make it grow.

Hickory, Dickory, Dock

HICKORY, dickory, dock,
The mouse ran up the clock.
The clock struck one,
The mouse ran down,
Hickory, dickory, dock.

A Dillar, a Dollar

A dillar, a dollar,
A ten o'clock scholar,
What makes you come so soon?
You used to come at ten o'clock,
But now you come at noon.

Girls and Boys Come Out to Play

GIRLS and boys come out to play
The moon it shines as bright as day.
Leave your supper and leave your sleep
And come with your playfellows into the street;
Come with a whoop and come with a call,
Come with a goodwill, or come not at all;
Up the ladder and down the wall,
A halfpenny loaf will serve us all.
You find milk and I'll find flour,
And we'll have pudding in half an hour.

Row, Row, Row the Boat

Row, row, row the boat
Gently down the stream,
Merrily, merrily, merrily, merrily,
Life is but a dream.

I Had a Little Nut Tree

I had a little nut tree and nothing would it bear
But a silver nutmeg and a golden pear.
The King of Spain's daughter came to visit me
And all for the sake of my little nut tree.
I danced over the water, I danced over the sea
But all the birds of the air couldn't catch me.

Sally Go Round the Sun

SALLY go round the sun
Sally go round the moon
Sally go round the chimney pots
On a Saturday afternoon.

Pat-a-Cake, Pat-a-Cake

PAT-a-cake, pat-a-cake,
Baker's man,
Bake me a cake
As fast as you can.
Pat it and prick it
And mark it with B,
And put it in the oven
For Baby and me.

Mix a Pancake

MIX a pancake,
Stir a pancake,
Pop it in the pan.

Fry the pancake,
Toss the pancake,
Catch it if you can!

One Potato,
Two Potato

ONE potato, two potato,
Three potato, four,
Five potato, six potato,
Seven potato, more!

Jelly on the Plate

JELLY on the plate,
Jelly on the plate.
Wibble, wobble,
Wibble, wobble,
Jelly on the plate.

The Wheels on the Bus

THE wheels on the bus go round and round,
Round and round, round and round.
The wheels on the bus go round and round,
All day long.

Round and Round
the Garden

ROUND and round the garden
Like a teddy bear;
One step, two step,
Tickle you under there!

Little Arabella Miller

LITTLE Arabella Miller
Had a fuzzy caterpillar.
First it climbed upon her mother,
Then upon her baby brother.
They said, "Arabella Miller,
Put away your caterpillar!"

What Do You Suppose?

WHAT do you suppose?
A bee sat on my nose.
Then what do you think?
He gave me a wink
And said, "I beg your pardon,
I thought you were the garden."

Little Bo-Peep

LITTLE Bo-Peep has lost her sheep,
And doesn't know where to find them;
Leave them alone, and they'll come home,
Bringing their tails behind them.

Little Bo-Peep fell fast asleep,
And dreamt she heard them bleating;
But when she awoke she found it a joke,
For still they all were fleeting.

Then up she took her little crook,
Determined for to find them;
She found 'em indeed, but it made her heart bleed,
For they'd left their tails behind 'em.

It happened one day, as Bo-Peep did stray
Unto a meadow hard by,
There she espied their tails, side by side,
All hung on a tree to dry.

She heaved a sigh, and wiped her eye,
And ran o'er hill and dale-o,
And tried what she could, as a shepherdess should,
To tack to each sheep its tail-o.

JESSIE WILLCOX SMITH

Hush-a-bye, Baby

Hush–a–bye, baby, on the tree top,
When the wind blows, the cradle will rock;
When the bough bends, the cradle will fall.
Down will come baby, cradle, and all.

One, Two, Buckle My Shoe

ONE, two, buckle my shoe;
Three, four, shut the door;
Five, six, pick up sticks;
Seven, eight, lay them straight;
Nine, ten, a good fat hen;
Eleven, twelve, dig and delve;
Thirteen, fourteen, maids a-courting;
Fifteen, sixteen, maids a-kissing;
Seventeen, eighteen, maids a-waiting;
Nineteen, twenty, my plate's empty.

Diddle, Diddle, Dumpling

DIDDLE, diddle, dumpling, my son John,
Went to bed with his trousers on;
One shoe off, and one shoe on,
Diddle, diddle, dumpling, my son John.

Little Jack Horner

LITTLE Jack Horner
Sat in a corner,
Eating his Christmas pie;
He put in his thumb,
And pulled out a plum,
And said, "What a good boy am I!"

Grey Goose

GREY goose and gander,
Waft your wings together,
And carry the good king's daughter
Over the one-strand river.

Terence McDiddler

TERENCE McDiddler,
  The three-stringed fiddler,
Can charm, if you please,
The fish from the seas.

Old King Cole

OLD King Cole was a merry old soul,
And a merry old soul was he;
And he called for his pipe,
And he called for his bowl,
And he called for his fiddlers three.
And every fiddler, he had a fine fiddle,
And a very fine fiddle had he;
"Tweedle dee, tweedle dee," said the fiddlers:
"Oh, there's none so rare as can compare
With King Cole and his fiddlers three."

The Grand Old Duke of York

OH, the grand old Duke of York,
He had ten thousand men;
He marched them up to the top of the hill
And he marched them down again.
And when they were up, they were up,
And when they were down, they were down,
And when they were only halfway up,
They were neither up nor down.

Diddlety, Diddlety, Dumpty

DIDDLETY, diddlety, dumpty;
The cat ran up the plum-tree.
Half-a-crown
To fetch her down;
Diddlety, diddlety, dumpty.

Rain, Rain, Go to Spain

RAIN, rain, go to Spain,
Don't come back again!

Monday's Child

MONDAY'S child is fair of face;
Tuesday's child is full of grace;
Wednesday's child is full of woe;
Thursday's child has far to go;
Friday's child is loving and giving;
Saturday's child must work for a living,
But the child who is born on the Sabbath day
Is bonny and blithe and good and gay.

Little Tommy Tucker

LITTLE Tommy Tucker,
He sang for his supper.
What did he sing for?
Why, white bread and butter.
How can I cut it without a knife?
How can I marry without a wife?

Jumping Joan

Here am I
Little Jumping Joan;

When nobody's with me
I'm all alone.

Upon Paul's Steeple

UPON Paul's steeple stands a tree
As full of apples as may be;
The little boys of London Town
They run with hooks to pull them down;
And then they run from hedge to hedge,
Until they come to London Bridge.

Little Boy Blue

LITTLE boy blue, come blow your horn;
The sheep's in the meadow, the cow's in the corn.
Where's the little boy that looks after the sheep?
He's under a haystack, fast asleep.
Will you wake him? No, not I;
For if I do, he'll be sure to cry.

Three Blind Mice

THREE blind mice,
See how they run!
They all ran after the farmer's wife,
Who cut off their tails with a carving knife;
Did ever you hear such a thing in your life
As three blind mice?

I Saw a Ship

I saw a ship a-sailing
A-sailing on the sea;
And, oh! it was all laden
With pretty things for me!

There were comfits in the cabin,
And apples in the hold;
The sails were made of silk,
And the masts were made of gold.

The four-and-twenty sailors
That stood between the decks,
Were four-and-twenty white mice
With chains about their necks.

The captain was a duck,
With a packet on his back;
And when the ship began to move,
The captain said, "Quack! Quack!"

Lavender's Blue, Dilly Dilly

LAVENDER'S blue, dilly dilly,
Lavender's green;
When I am king, dilly, dilly,
You shall be queen.

There Was a Little Dog

THERE was a little dog and he had a little tail
And he used to wag, wag, wag it!
But when he was sad, because he had been bad,
On the ground he would drag, drag, drag it!

Me

I look in the mirror
And what do I see?
I see myself
Looking at me!

NOLA WOOD

Hair Ribbons

I'M three years old and like to wear,
A bow of ribbon on my hair.
Sometimes it's pink, sometimes it's blue;
I think it's pretty there, don't you?

Hair

THERE'S
Curly hair
Straight hair
Fine hair
Strong.
Black hair
Blonde hair
Short hair
Long.
Who cares
If my hair's
Every sort of wrong?
Hair!
Wash it
Dry it
Brush it
Part it
Comb it
Plait it –
            There!

DOROTHY MILLS

Mornings Are for Laces

DANIEL puts
His shoes on last.
Although he tries
He can't tie laces
Very fast.

Still,
He likes
Those
Nearly new,
Red
Orange
Yellow
Blue,
Green
Indigo
Violet
Rainbow-coloured laces.

If he pulls them
From his shoes
And twists them round
His fingers,
They become bright,
Squirmy,
Wriggly worms.
And,
He can turn those laces
Into
Smiling,
Frowning,
Sad
Or clowning
Faces.

Mornings are best
For doing things with laces;
Before they've had the time
To get tied up in shoes.

BILL NAGELKERKE

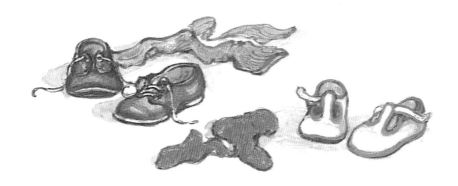

Shoes

RED shoes, blue shoes,
Old shoes, new shoes,
Shoes that are black,
Shoes that are white,
Shoes that are loose,
Shoes that are tight.
Shoes with buckles,
Shoes with bows,
Shoes that are narrow
And pinch your toes.

Shoes that are yellow,
Shoes that are green,
Shoes that are dirty,
Shoes that are clean.
Shoes for cold weather,
Shoes for when it's hot.
Shoes with laces
That get tangled in a knot!

JOHN FOSTER

Girl Friends

Marian, Lily and Annie Rose
Are three bonny girls, as everyone knows.
Sometimes bouncy, sometimes sad,
Sometimes sleepy, sometimes glad,
Sometimes grubby, sometimes clean,
Often kind, though sometimes mean.
But most of the time they try to be good,
And to all that know them it's understood
That Marian, Lily and Annie Rose
Are best of friends, as everyone knows.

SHIRLEY HUGHES

Little Girl, Little Girl

Little girl, little girl, where have you been?
Gathering roses to give to the Queen.
Little girl, little girl, what gave she you?
She gave me a diamond as big as my shoe.

The Months

January brings the snow,
Makes our feet and fingers glow.

February brings the rain,
Thaws the frozen lake again.

March brings breezes loud and shrill,
Stirs the dancing daffodil.

April brings the primrose sweet,
Scatters daisies at our feet.

May brings flocks of pretty lambs,
Skipping by their fleecy dams.

June brings tulips, lilies, roses,
Fills the children's hands with posies.

Hot July brings cooling showers,
Apricots and gillyflowers.

August brings the sheaves of corn,
Then the harvest home is borne.

Warm September brings the fruit,
Sportsmen then begin to shoot.

Fresh October brings the pheasant,
Then to gather nuts is pleasant.

Dull November brings the blast,
Then the leaves are whirling fast.

Chill December brings the sleet,
Blazing fire, and Christmas treat.

SARA COLERIDGE

A Spike of Green

WHEN I went out
The sun was hot,
It shone upon
My flower pot.

And there I saw
A spike of green
That no one else
Had ever seen!

On other days
The things I see
Are mostly old
Except for me.

But this green spike
So new and small
Had never yet
Been seen at all.

BARBARA BAKER

Balloons...Balloons

BALLOONS, balloons
on coloured string
are blowing out
into the Spring.

Balloons, balloons
filled up with air
are sailing off
to everywhere.

Balloons, balloons
all bright and round
are floating up
without a sound.

MYRA COHN LIVINGSTON

Duck Weather

SPLISHING, splashing in the rain,
Up the street and back again,
Stomping, stamping through the flood,
We don't mind a bit of mud.
Running pavements, gutters flowing,
All the cars with wipers going,
We don't care about the weather,
Tramping hand in hand together.
We don't mind a damp wet day,
Sloshing puddles all the way,
Splishing, splashing in the rain,
Up the street and back again.

SHIRLEY HUGHES

The Rain

THE rain is raining all around,
It falls on field and tree;
It rains on the umbrellas here
And on the ships at sea.

ROBERT LOUIS STEVENSON

To Walk in Warm Rain

TO walk in warm rain
And get wetter and wetter!
To do it again –
To walk in warm rain
Till you drip like a drain.
To walk in warm rain
And get wetter and wetter.

DAVID McCORD

Winter Days

BITING air
Winds blow
City streets
Under snow

Noses red
Lips sore
Runny eyes
Hands raw

Chimneys smoke
Cars crawl
Piled snow
On garden wall

Slush in gutters
Ice in lanes
Frosty patterns
On window panes

Morning call
Lift up head
Nipped by winter
Stay in bed

GARETH OWEN

The Park

I'M glad that I
Live near a park

For in the winter
After dark

The park lights shine
As bright and still

As dandelions
On a hill.

JAMES S. TIPPETT

Little Wind

LITTLE wind, blow on the hill-top,
Little wind, blow down the plain;
Little wind, blow up the sunshine,
Little wind, blow off the rain.

KATE GREENAWAY

Wind Song

WHEN the wind blows
The quiet things speak.
Some whisper, some clang,
Some creak.

Grasses swish.
Treetops sigh.
Flags slap
and snap at the sky.
Wires on poles
whistle and hum.
Ashcans roll.
Windows drum.

When the wind goes –
suddenly
then,
the quiet things
are quiet again.

LILIAN MOORE

The Magic Seeds

THERE was an old woman who sowed a corn seed,
And from it there sprouted a tall yellow weed.
She planted the seeds of the tall yellow flower,
And up sprang a blue one in less than an hour.
The seed of the blue one she sowed in a bed,
And up sprang a tall tree with blossoms of red.
And high in the tree-top there sang a white bird,
And his song was the sweetest that ever was heard.
The people they came from far and near,
The song of the little white bird to hear.

JAMES REEVES

Christmas Is Coming

CHRISTMAS is coming,
The geese are getting fat,
Please to put a penny
In the old man's hat.
If you haven't got a penny,
A ha'penny will do;
If you haven't got a ha'penny,
Then God bless you!

The Children's Carol

HERE we come again, again, and here we come again,
Christmas is a single pearl swinging on a chain,
Christmas is a single flower in a barren wood,
Christmas is a single sail on the salty flood,
Christmas is a single star in the empty sky,
Christmas is a single song sung for charity.
Here we come again, again, to sing to you again,
Give a single penny that we may not sing in vain.

ELEANOR FARJEON

Question Time

*W*HAT *does a monster look like?*
   Well…hairy
and scary,
and furry
and burly and pimply and dimply and warty and naughty and wrinkled and
crinkled…
That's what a monster looks like.

How does a monster move?
It oozes,
it shambles,
it crawls and it ambles, it slouches and shuffles and trudges, it lumbers
and toddles, it creeps and it waddles…
That's how a monster moves.

Where does a monster live?
In garden sheds,
under beds,
in wardrobes, in plug holes and ditches,
beneath city streets, just under your feet…
That's where a monster lives.

How does a monster eat?
It slurps and it burps and gobbles and gulps and sips and swallows and
scoffs, it nibbles and munches, it chews and it crunches…
That's how a monster eats.

What does a monster eat?
Slugs and bats and bugs and rats and stones and mud and bones and blood
and squelchy squids…and nosy kids.
YUM!
That's what a monster eats!

MICHAELA MORGAN

The Toaster

A silver-scaled Dragon with jaws flaming red
Sits at my elbow and toasts my bread.
I hand him fat slices, and then, one by one,
He hands them back when he sees they are done.

WILLIAM JAY SMITH

A Baby Sardine

A baby sardine
Saw her first submarine:
She was scared and watched through a peephole.

"Oh come, come, come,"
Said the sardine's mum.
"It's only a tin full of people."

SPIKE MILLIGAN

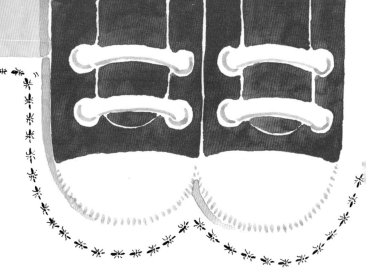

Ants
Live Here

ANTS live here
by the curb stone,
see?
They worry a lot
about giants like me.

LILIAN MOORE

Wasps

WASPS like coffee.
Syrup.
Tea.
Coca-Cola.
Butter.
Me.

DOROTHY ALDIS

73

The Tickle Rhyme

"WHO'S that tickling my back?" said the wall.
"Me," said a small
caterpillar. "I'm learning
to crawl."

IAN SERRAILLIER

My Dog

MY dog is such a gentle soul,
Although he's big it's true.
He brings the paper in his mouth,
He brings the postman too.

MAX FATCHEN

Min

I'VE got a dog
Whose name is Min,
As soon as she's out
She wants to come in.

She growls,
She howls,
She bumps,
She thumps,
She paws,
She claws,

And, finally, Min gets in.

BARBARA IRESON

Through the Jungle the Elephant Goes

THROUGH the jungle the elephant goes,
Swaying his trunk to and fro,
Munching, crunching, tearing trees,
Stamping seeds, eating leaves.
His eyes are small, his feet are fat,
Hey, elephant, don't do that!

De Beat

DE beat of de drum
is a living heart

De skin of de drum
is a living goat

De wood of de drum
is a living tree

De belly of de drum
is de call of de sea

De dum of de drum is me

GRACE NICHOLS

Cat in the Dark

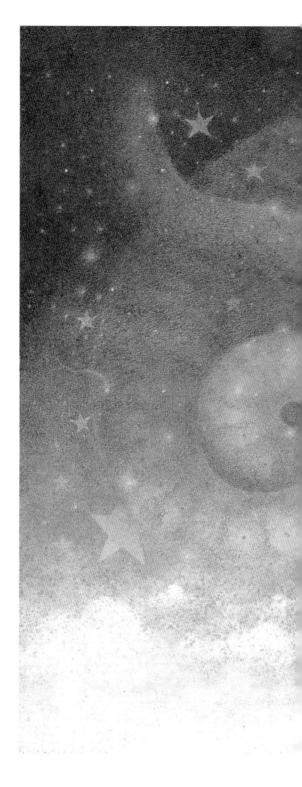

MOTHER, Mother what was that?
Hush my darling! Only the cat!
(Fighty-bitey, ever-so-mighty)
Out in the moony dark.

Mother, Mother what was that?
Hush my darling! Only the cat!
(Prowley-yowley, sleepy-creepy,
Fighty-bitey, ever-so-mighty)
Out in the moony dark.

Mother, Mother what was that?
Hush my darling! Only the cat!
(Sneaky-peeky, cosy-dozey,
Prowley-yowley, sleepy-creepy,
Fighty-bitey, ever-so-mighty)
Out in the moony dark.

Mother, Mother what was that?
Hush my darling! Only the cat!
(Patchy-scratchy, furry-purry,
Sneaky-peeky, cosy-dozey,
Prowley-yowley, sleepy-creepy,
Fighty-bitey, ever-so-mighty)
Out in the moony dark.

MARGARET MAHY

Night Flight

ANNIE flew out of the window,
Bedclothes and cot and all,
And floated around above the ground,
And over the garden wall.

And her shadow skimmed over the gardens
And followed her all the way,
As she looked down on the roofs of the town
And the moon shone as bright as day.

SHIRLEY HUGHES

Witch, Witch

"Witch, witch, where do you fly?"...
    "Under the clouds and over the sky."

"Witch, witch, what do you eat?"...
"Little black apples from Hurricane Street."

"Witch, witch, what do you drink?"...
"Vinegar, blacking and good red ink."

"Witch, witch, where do you sleep?"...
"Up in the clouds where pillows are cheap."

ROSE FYLEMAN

Mrs Moon

Mrs Moon
sitting up in the sky
little old lady
rock-a-bye
with a ball of fading light
and silvery needles
knitting the night

ROGER McGOUGH

The Coming of Teddy Bears

THE air is quiet
Round my bed.
The dark is drowsy
In my head.
The sky's forgetting
To be red,
And soon I'll be asleep.

A half a million
Miles away
The silver stars
Come out to play,
And comb their hair
And that's OK
And soon I'll be asleep.

And teams of fuzzy
Teddy bears
Are stumping slowly
Up the stairs
To rock me in
Their rocking chairs
And soon I'll be asleep.

The night is shining
Round my head.
The room is snuggled
In my bed.
Tomorrow I'll be
Big they said
And soon I'll be asleep.

DENNIS LEE

Listen to the Tree Bear

LISTEN to the tree bear
  Crying in the night
Crying for his mammy
In the pale moonlight.

What will his mammy do
When she hears him cry?
She'll tuck him in a cocoa-pod
And sing a lullaby.

83

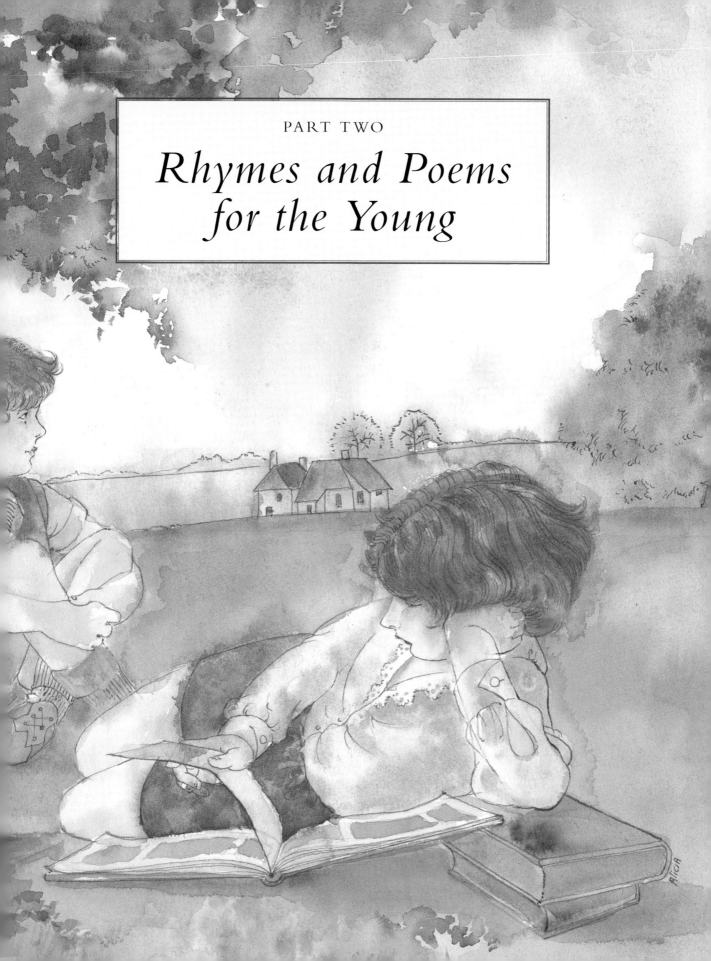

PART TWO

Rhymes and Poems for the Young

Monday's Child
Is Red and Spotty

M ONDAY'S child is red and spotty,
Tuesday's child won't use the potty.
Wednesday's child won't go to bed,
Thursday's child will not be fed.
Friday's child breaks all his toys,
Saturday's child makes an awful noise.
And the child that's born on the seventh day
Is a pain in the neck like the rest, OK!

COLIN McNAUGHTON

Where Did
the Baby Go?

I cannot remember –
And neither can my mother –
Just when it was our baby
Turned into my brother.

JULIE HOLDER

Picking Noses

WHEN I was young
I picked my nose.
I just said,
"Gimme one of those!"

Now I've gone off
The one I chose;
You wouldn't swap,
I don't suppose?

COLIN McNAUGHTON

Second Best

I never get anything new.
With three older brothers,
My clothes come from others.
Does this ever happen to you?

IAN LARMONT

My Sister Laura

My sister Laura's bigger than me
And lifts me up quite easily.
I can't lift her, I've tried and tried;
She must have something heavy inside.

SPIKE MILLIGAN

Brother

I had a little brother
And I brought him to my mother
And I said I want another
Little brother for a change.
But she said don't be a bother
So I took him to my father
And I said this little bother
Of a brother's very strange.

But he said one little brother
Is exactly like another
And every little brother
Misbehaves a bit he said.
So I took the little bother
From my mother and my father
And I put the little bother
Of a brother back to bed.

MARY ANN HOBERMAN

from *A Song About Myself*

THERE was a naughty boy,
  A naughty boy was he,
He would not stop at home,
  He could not quiet be –
    He took
    In his knapsack
    A book
    Full of vowels
    And a shirt
    With some towels –
    A slight cap
    For a night-cap –
    A hair brush,
    Comb ditto,
    New stockings,
    For old ones
    Would split O!
    This knapsack
    Tight at's back
    He riveted close
And followed his nose
    To the North,
    To the North,
And followed his nose
    To the North.

JOHN KEATS

90

There Was a Little Girl

THERE was a little girl, who had a little curl
  Right in the middle of her forehead,
And when she was good, she was very, very good,
But when she was bad she was horrid.

HENRY WADSWORTH LONGFELLOW

Going Through the Old Photos

WHO'S that?
    That's your Auntie Mabel
and that's me
under the table.

Who's that?
That's Uncle Billy.
Who's that?
Me being silly.

Who's that
licking a lolly?
I'm not sure
but I think it's Polly.

Who's that
behind the tree?
I don't know,
I can't see.
Could be you.
Could be me.

Who's that?
Baby Joe.
Who's that?
I don't know.

Who's that standing
on his head?
Turn it round.
It's Uncle Ted.

MICHAEL ROSEN

Goodbye Granny

GOODBYE Granny
it's nearly time to fly
goodbye Granny
I am going in the sky.
I have my suitcase
and things.
You have packed
me everything
except the sunshine.
All our good times
are stored
up inside
more than enough
for any plane ride.
Goodbye Granny
things will be all right
goodbye Granny
I won't forget to write.
Goodbye Granny
bye! bye!
bye! bye!

PAULINE STEWART

Newcomers

MY father came to England
from another country
my father's mother came to England
from another country
but my father's father
stayed behind.

So my dad had no dad here
and I never saw him at all.

One day in spring
some things arrived:
a few old papers,
a few old photos
and – oh yes –
a hulky bulky thick checked jacket
that belonged to the man
I would have called "Grandad".
The Man Who Stayed Behind.
But I kept that jacket
and I wore it
and I wore it
and I wore it
till it wore right through
at the back.

MICHAEL ROSEN

The Older
the Violin the
Sweeter the Tune

ME Granny old
Me Granny wise
stories shine like a moon
from inside she eyes.

Me Granny can dance
Me Granny can sing
but she can't play the violin.

Yet she always saying,
"Dih older dih violin
de sweeter de tune."

Me Granny must be wiser
than the man inside the moon.

JOHN AGARD

Dad and the Cat and the Tree

THIS morning a cat got
Stuck in our tree.
Dad said, "Right, just
Leave it to me."

The tree was wobbly,
The tree was tall.
Mum said, "For goodness'
Sake don't fall."

"Fall?" scoffed Dad,
"A climber like me?
Child's play, this is!
You wait and see."

He got out the ladder
From the garden shed.
It slipped. He landed
In the flower bed.

"Never mind," said Dad,
Brushing the dirt
Off his hair and his face
And his trousers and his shirt,

"We'll try Plan B. Stand
Out of the way!"
Mum said, "Don't fall
Again, OK?"

"Fall again?" said Dad.
"Funny joke!"
Then he swung himself up
On a branch. It broke.

Dad landed *wallop*
Back on the deck.
Mum said, "Stop it,
You'll break your neck!"

"Rubbish!" said Dad.
"Now we'll try Plan C.
Easy as winking
To a climber like me!"

Then he climbed up high
On the garden wall.
Guess what?
He *didn't fall*!

He gave a great leap
And he landed flat
In the crook of the tree-trunk —
Right on the cat!

The cat gave a yell
And sprang to the ground,
Pleased as Punch to be
Safe and sound.

So it's smiling and smirking,
Smug as can be,
But poor old Dad's
Still

Stuck
Up
The
Tree!

KIT WRIGHT

Back-to-School Blues

HAIR'S been cut. It's neat again.
Got socks and shoes on my feet again.
Saddled with a bag as new as my shoes,
I got the mean ol' back-to-school blues.

ELIZABETH HONEY

I Don't Want to Go into School

I don't want to go into school today, Mum,
I don't feel like schoolwork today.
Oh, don't make me go into school today, Mum,
Oh, please let me stay home and play.

But you must go to school, my cherub, my lamb.
If you don't it will be a disaster.
How would they manage without you, my sweet,
After all, you are the headmaster!

COLIN McNAUGHTON

Where Do Teachers Go?

AT the end of the day, where do teachers go?
Do they ride horses in a wild west show?
Do they climb mountains, covered in snow?
Do they jump into boats and learn to row?
Do they sing in voices, high and low?
Do they plant flowers and hope they'll grow?
Don't ask me, because I don't know.

JOHN COLDWELL

Accidentally

Once – I didn't mean to,
but that
was that –
I yawned in the sunshine
and swallowed a gnat.

I'd rather eat mushrooms
and bullfrogs' legs,
I'd rather have pepper
all over my eggs

than open my mouth
on a sleepy day
and close on a gnat
going down that way.

It tasted sort of salty.
It didn't hurt a bit.
I accidentally ate a gnat
and that
was
it!

MAXINE W. KUMIN

Drinking Fountain

Wʜᴇɴ I climb up
   To get a drink,
It doesn't work
The way you'd think.

I turn it up.
The water goes
And hits me right
Upon the nose.

I turn it down
To make it small
And don't get any
Drink at all.

MARCHETTE CHUTE

Peas

I eat my peas with honey,
I've done it all my life;
It makes the peas taste funny,
But it keeps them on the knife.

Sweet Tooth

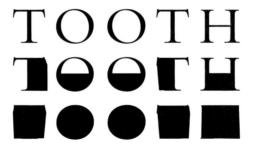

GINA DOUTHWAITE

Sweet Song

This is the sweet song,
Song of all the sweets,
Caramel and butterscotch
Bullseyes, raspberry treats;

Treacle toffee, acid drops,
Pastilles, crystal fruits,
Bubble-gum and liquorice-sticks
As black as new gum-boots;

Peppermint creams and aniseed balls,
Tiny sweets and whoppers,
Dolly-mixtures, chocolate drops,
Gigantic gob-stoppers;

Lemon sherbets, jelly babies,
Chocolate cream and flake,
Nougat, fudge and such as give
You tooth- and belly-ache.

VERNON SCANNELL

The Man Who Wasn't There

YESTERDAY upon the stair
I met a man who wasn't there;
He wasn't there again today,
I wish, I wish, he'd go away.

I've seen his shapeless shadow-coat
Beneath the stairway, hanging about;
And outside, muffled in a cloak
The same colour as the dark;

I've seen him in a black, black suit
Shaking, under the broken light;
I've seen him swim across the floor
And disappear beneath the door;

And once, I almost heard his breath
Behind me, running up the path;
Inside he leant against the wall,
And turned…and was no one at all.

Yesterday upon the stair
I met the man who wasn't there;
He wasn't there again today,
I wish, I wish, he'd go away.

BRIAN LEE

Wobble-dee-woo

WHAT would you do
With a Wobble-dee-woo?
Would you eat it
Or wear it
Or play it?
What would you do
With a Wobble-dee-woo?
(I've only just learned
How to say it.)

What would you do
With a Wobble-dee-woo?
Would you wear it
Or play it
Or eat it?
What would you do
With a Wobble-dee-woo?
(I'm sorry, I'll have
To repeat it.)

What would you do
With a Wobble-dee-woo?
Would you play it
Or eat it
Or wear it?
What would you do
With a Wobble-dee-woo?
(It's driving me mad,
I can't bear it!)

COLIN WEST

Doin' The Pig

YOU can skip, step and scamper
you can jive, jump and jig
you can do the boogy-woogy
but can you do The Pig?

You get down on your hands and knees
put your nose to the ground.
You grunt and squeal, and squeal and grunt
and gallop round and round.

You can do
you can do
you can do The Pig

You can do
you can do
you can do the Big Pink Pig

MICHAEL ROSEN

Flight of Fancy

Poor, pestered parents often sigh:
"You'll get your wish when pigs can fly!"
Well then, how wonderful to see
A pig-flock rising from a tree;
High-flying porkers on the way
To Bali, Boston or Bombay,
Honking like geese, though maybe not as
Graceful upon their flapping trotters.
How we would cheer to see them rise
Fitly and fatly to the skies,
Knowing, whatever route they'd taken,
These soaring sows had saved our bacon!

HAZEL TOWNSON

Jim

Down behind the dustbin
I met a dog called Jim.
He didn't know me
and I didn't know him.

MICHAEL ROSEN

A Young Man from Berwick-on-Tweed

A young man from Berwick-on-Tweed
Kept a very strange thing on a lead.
He was never once seen
To give it a clean
Or anything else it might need.

MICHAEL PALIN

A Tortoise Called Joe

THERE once was a tortoise called Joe
Whose progress was painfully slow.
He'd stop for a week,
Look around, take a peek,
Then, unlike a shot, off he'd go.

MICHAEL PALIN

Pelican / Toucan

"CAN you do this?" says Pelican,
His large beak gaping wide.
"Who needs to," says the Toucan
As he turns round goggle-eyed.
"It only means that you can
Hold a lot more air inside."

BERT KITCHEN

Seal

SEE how he dives
From the rocks with a zoom!
See how he darts
Through his watery room
Past crabs and eels
And green seaweed,
Past fluffs of sandy
Minnow feed!
See how he swims
With a swerve and a twist,
A flip of the flipper,
A flick of the wrist!
Quicksilver-quick,
Softer than spray,
Down he plunges
And sweeps away;
Before you can think,
Before you can utter
Words like "Dill pickle"
Or "Apple butter",
Back up he swims
Past Sting Ray and Shark,
Out with a zoom,
A whoop, a bark;
Before you can say
Whatever you wish,
He plops at your side
With a mouthful of fish!

WILLIAM JAY SMITH

The Common Cormorant

THE common cormorant or shag
Lays eggs inside a paper bag.
The reason you will see no doubt
It is to keep the lightning out.
But what those unobservant birds
Have never noticed is that herds
Of wandering bears may come with buns
And steal the bags to hold the crumbs.

CHRISTOPHER ISHERWOOD

Who's There?

IF you hear a dinosaur
Knocking loudly on your door,
Through the keyhole firmly say,
"Nobody is home today."
If the bell should start to ring,
Tell the beast, "No visiting."
If you see there's more than one,
Turn around and start to run.

MAX FATCHEN

Do Not Disturb the Dinosaur

Do not disturb the dinosaur

who's fast asleep upon the floor

between one country

and another.

Climb him and you'll

soon discover

that tickling makes him twitch and w

...d scratch and cause a great earthquake and yawn a whirlwind round the world. He's better off asleep, all curled, or stretched out, smiling, for a change, pretending he's a mountain range.

GINA DOUTHWAITE

Mice

I think mice
Are rather nice.

Their tails are long,
Their faces small,
They haven't any
Chins at all.
Their ears are pink,
Their teeth are white,
They run about
The house at night.
They nibble things
They shouldn't touch
And no one seems
To like them much.

But I think mice
Are nice.

ROSE FYLEMAN

116

Cats

CATS sleep
Anywhere,
Any table,
Any chair,
Top of piano,
Window-ledge,
In the middle,
On the edge,
Open drawer,
Empty shoe,
Anybody's
Lap will do,

Fitted in a
Cardboard box,
In the cupboard
With your frocks –
Anywhere!
They don't care!
Cats sleep
Anywhere.

ELEANOR FARJEON

Alligator

IF you want to see an alligator
you must go down to the muddy slushy end
of the old Caroony River

I know an alligator
who's living down there
She's a-big. She's a-mean. She's a-wild.
She's a-fierce.

But if you really want to see an alligator
you must go down to the muddy slushy end
of the old Caroony River

Go down gently to that river and say
"Alligator Mama
Alligator Mama
Alligator Mamaaaaaaa"

And up she'll rise
but don't stick around
RUN FOR YOUR LIFE

GRACE NICHOLS

Pirate Captain Jim

"WALK the plank," says Pirate Jim.
    "But Captain Jim, I cannot swim."
"Then you must steer us through the gale."
"But Captain Jim, I cannot sail."
"Then down with the galley slaves you go."
"But Captain Jim I cannot row."
"Then you must be the pirate's clerk."
"But Captain Jim I cannot work."
"Then a pirate captain you must be."
"Thank you, Jim," says Captain Me.

SHEL SILVERSTEIN

The Sea-Monster's Snack

DEEP down upon his sandy bed
the monster turned his slimy head,
grinned and licked his salty lips
and ate another bag of ships.

CHARLES THOMSON

Undersea

BENEATH the waters
Green and cool
The mermaids keep
A swimming school.

The oysters trot;
The lobsters prance;
The dolphins come
To join the dance.

But the jellyfish
Who are rather small,
Can't seem to learn
The steps at all.

MARCHETTE CHUTE

Sea Timeless Song

HURRICANE come
and hurricane go
but sea…sea timeless
    sea timeless

    sea timeless

    sea timeless

    sea timeless.

Hibiscus bloom
then dry-wither so
but sea…sea timeless
    sea timeless

    sea timeless

    sea timeless

    sea timeless.

Tourist come
and tourist go
but sea…sea timeless
    sea timeless

    sea timeless

    sea timeless

    sea timeless.

GRACE NICHOLS

Haiku

SHIMMERING heat waves,
A hot pebble in the hand,
Light-dance on the sea.

WENDY COPE

What Is Red?

R<small>ED</small> is a sunset
Blazing and bright.
Red is feeling brave
With all your might.
Red is a sunburn
Spot on your nose.
Sometimes red
Is a red, red rose.
Red squiggles out
When you cut your hand.
Red is a brick and
The sound of a band.
Red is a hotness
You get inside
When you're embarrassed
And want to hide.
Firecracker, fire-engine
Fire-flicker red –
And when you're angry
Red runs through your head.
Red is an Indian,
A valentine heart,
The trimming on
A circus cart.

Red is a lipstick,
Red is a shout,
Red is a signal
That says: "Watch out!"
Red is a great big
Rubber ball.
Red is the giant-est
Colour of all.
Red is a show-off
No doubt about it –
But can you imagine
Living without it?

MARY O'NEILL

The Sun

THE sun is a glowing spider
that crawls out
from under the earth
to make her way across the sky
warming and weaving
with her bright old fingers
of light.

GRACE NICHOLS

Yellow

YELLOW for melons.
Yellow for sun.
Yellow for buttercups,
Picked one by one.

The yolk of an egg
Is yellow, too.
And sometimes clouds
Have a daffodil hue.

Bananas are yellow
And candleshine.
What's your favourite colour?
Yellow is mine.

OLIVE DOVE

The Pines

HEAR the rumble,
Oh, hear the crash.
The great trees tumble.
The strong boughs smash.

Men with saws
Are cutting the pines –
That marched like soldiers
In straight green lines.

Seventy years
Have made them tall.
It takes ten minutes
To make them fall.

And breaking free
With never a care,
The pine cones leap
Through the clear, bright air.

MARGARET MAHY

Where Go the Boats?

DARK brown is the river,
Golden is the sand.
It flows along for ever,
With trees on either hand.

Green leaves a–floating,
Castles of the foam,
Boats of mine a–boating –
Where will all come home?

On goes the river
And out past the mill,
Away down the valley,
Away down the hill.

Away down the river,
A hundred miles or more,
Other little children
Shall bring my boats ashore.

ROBERT LOUIS STEVENSON

The Spinning Earth

THE earth, they say,
spins round and round.
It doesn't look it
from the ground,
and never makes
a spinning sound.

And water never
swirls and swishes
from oceans full
of dizzy fishes,
and shelves don't lose
their pans and dishes.

And houses don't go whirling by,
or puppies swirl around the sky,
or robins spin instead of fly.

It may be true
what people say
about one spinning
night and day...
but I keep wondering, anyway.

AILEEN FISHER

130

Holes of Green

TREES are full of holes —
between the leaves I mean.
But if you stand away enough
the holes fill up with green.

AILEEN FISHER

from *The Song of Solomon*

For, lo, the winter is past,
The rain is over and gone;
The flowers appear on the earth;
The time of the singing of birds is come,
And the voice of the turtle is heard in our land;
The fig tree putteth forth her green figs,
And the vines with the tender grape
Give a good smell.

THE BIBLE (*King James version*)

This Is the Key

THIS is the key of the kingdom:
In that kingdom there is a city.
In that city there is a town.
In that town there is a street.
In that street there is a lane.
In that lane there is a yard.
In that yard there is a house.
In that house there is a room.
In that room there is a bed.
On that bed there is a basket.
In that basket there are some flowers.

Flowers in a basket.
Basket on the bed.
Bed in the room.
Room in the house.
House in the yard.
Yard in the lane.
Lane in the street.
Street in the town.
Town in the city.
City in the kingdom.
Of the kingdom this is the key.

The Secret Song

WHO saw the petals
    drop from the rose?
I, said the spider,
But nobody knows.

Who saw the sunset
    flash on a bird?
I, said the fish,
But nobody heard.

Who saw the fog
    come over the sea?
I, said the sea pigeon,
Only me.

Who saw the first
    green light of the sun?
I, said the night owl,
The only one.

Who saw the moss
    creep over the stone?
I, said the grey fox,
All alone.

MARGARET WISE BROWN

Sing a Song of People

SING a song of people
Walking fast or slow;
People in the city
Up and down they go.

People on the sidewalk,
People on the bus;
People passing, passing,
In back and front of us.
People on the subway
Underneath the ground;
People riding taxis
Round and round and round.

People with their hats on,
Going in the doors;
People with umbrellas
When it rains and pours.
People in tall buildings
And in stores below;
Riding elevators
Up and down they go.

People walking singly,
People in a crowd;
People saying nothing,
People talking loud.
People laughing, smiling,
Grumpy people too;
People who just hurry
And never look at you!

Sing a song of people
Who like to come and go;
Sing of city people
You see but never know!

LOIS LENSKI

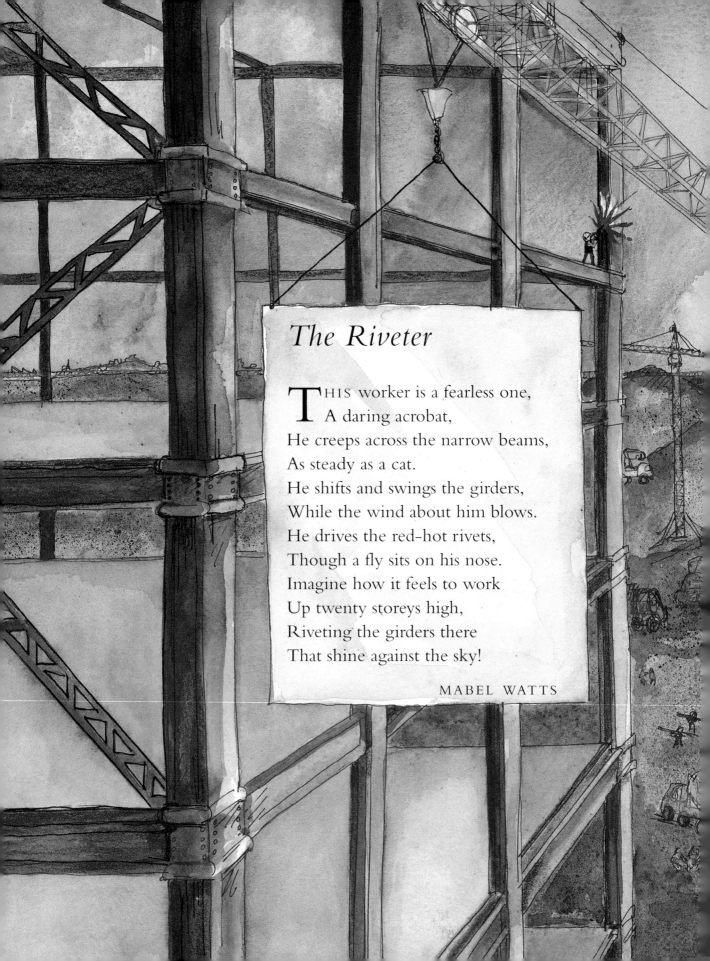

The Riveter

THIS worker is a fearless one,
  A daring acrobat,
He creeps across the narrow beams,
As steady as a cat.
He shifts and swings the girders,
While the wind about him blows.
He drives the red-hot rivets,
Though a fly sits on his nose.
Imagine how it feels to work
Up twenty storeys high,
Riveting the girders there
That shine against the sky!

MABEL WATTS

Building Site

MEN in
Miles of mud;
A sloshing
Wash.

Oceans of mud;
A rain
Drain.

Men like brown slugs on the
Drowned, brown, rain-washed plain.
Straining cranes,
Bucking trucks;
For men – too muddy much!

Pounds of caked mud
Cling to each boot,
Mud ball-and-chain
In that brown rain drain –
How can they lift a foot?

But in the end
Houses do get built on the silt.

MARIAN LINES

George Washington

GEORGE Washington chopped down a tree
And couldn't tell a lie;
When questioned by his father, he
Confessed, "Yes, it was I."

But as he handed back the axe,
He added in defence:
"Good training, sir, for lumberjacks
Or would-be presidents."

COLIN WEST

Columbus

COLUMBUS very well knew that
The world was round, it wasn't flat,
And almost went hysterical
Just proving it was spherical.

COLIN WEST

Elizabeth I

ELIZABETH the First, I hear,
Was quite a fussy queen,
And had a hot bath once a year
To keep her body clean.

COLIN WEST

Ivan the Terrible

IVAN the Terrible,
The first Russian Tsar,
Was just about bearable,
Till he went too far.

COLIN WEST

When All the World
Is Full of Snow

I never know
just where to go,
when all the world
is full of snow.

I do not want
to make a track,
not even
to the shed and back.

I only want
to watch and wait,
while snow moths settle
on the gate,

and swarming frost flakes
fill the trees
with billions
of albino bees.

I want to watch
the snow swarms thin,
'til all my bees
have settled in,

and on the ice
the boulders ride,
like sleeping snow geese
on the tide.

I only want
myself to be
as silent as
a winter tree,

to hear the swirling
stillness grow,
when all the world
is full of snow.

N. M. BODECKER

A Snow and Ice Poem

OUR street is dead lazy
especially in winter.
Some mornings you wake up
and it's still lying there
saying nothing. Huddled
under its white counterpane.

But soon the lorries arrive
like angry mums,
pull back the blankets
and send it shivering
off to work.

ROGER McGOUGH

Winter Morning

WINTER is the king of showmen,
Turning tree stumps into snow men
And houses into birthday cakes
And spreading sugar over lakes.
Smooth and clean and frosty white,
The world looks good enough to bite.
That's the season to be young,
Catching snow flakes on your tongue.

Snow is snowy when it's snowing,
I'm sorry it's slushy when it's going.

OGDEN NASH

Snow Clouds

LIKE sulky polar bears
Clouds prowl across the winter sky
From cold and snowy northern lands
As though from icy lairs.

Soon snow begins to fall —
Small snippets of the whitest fur
And like the stealthy polar bear
It makes no sound at all.

DAPHNE LISTER

A Visit from St Nicholas

'Twas the night before Christmas, when all through the house
Not a creature was stirring, not even a mouse;
The stockings were hung by the chimney with care,
In hopes that St Nicholas soon would be there;
The children were nestled all snug in their beds,
While visions of sugar-plums danced in their heads;
And mamma in her 'kerchief, and I in my cap,
Had just settled our brains for a long winter's nap –
When out on the lawn there arose such a clatter,
I sprang from my bed to see what was the matter.
Away to the window I flew like a flash,
Tore open the shutters, and threw up the sash.
The moon, on the breast of the new-fallen snow,
Gave the lustre of midday to objects below;
When, what to my wondering eyes should appear,
But a miniature sleigh and eight tiny reindeer,
With a little old driver, so lively and quick,
I knew in a moment it must be St Nick.
More rapid than eagles his coursers they came,
And he whistled, and shouted, and called them by name:
"Now, *Dasher*! now, *Dancer*! now, *Prancer* and *Vixen*!
On, *Comet*! on, *Cupid*! on *Donder* and *Blitzen*!
To the top of the porch! to the top of the wall!
Now dash away! dash away! dash away all!"
As dry leaves that before the wild hurricane fly,
When they meet with an obstacle, mount to the sky;
So up to the house-top the coursers they flew
With the sleigh full of toys, and St Nicholas too.

And then, in a twinkling, I heard on the roof
The prancing and pawing of each little hoof –
As I drew in my head, and was turning around,
Down the chimney St Nicholas came with a bound.
He was dressed all in fur, from his head to his foot,
And his clothes were all tarnished with ashes and soot;
A bundle of toys he had flung on his back,
And he looked like a pedlar just opening his pack.
His eyes – how they twinkled; his dimples, how merry!
His cheeks were like roses, his nose like a cherry!
His droll little mouth was drawn up like a bow,
And the beard of his chin was as white as the snow;
The stump of a pipe he held tight in his teeth,
And the smoke it encircled his head like a wreath;
He had a broad face and a little round belly
That shook, when he laughed, like a bowl full of jelly.
He was chubby and plump, a right jolly old elf,
And I laughed when I saw him, in spite of myself;
A wink of his eye and a twist of his head
Soon gave me to know I had nothing to dread;
He spoke not a word, but went straight to his work,
And filled all the stockings; then turned with a jerk,
And laying his finger aside of his nose,
And giving a nod, up the chimney he rose;
He sprang to his sleigh, to his team gave a whistle,
And away they all flew like the down of a thistle.
But I heard him exclaim, ere he drove out of sight,
"Happy Christmas to all, and to all a good night!"

CLEMENT CLARKE MOORE

JESSIE WILLCOX SMITH,

The Remarkable Cake

It's Christmas – the time when we gather to make
A truly remarkable once-a-year cake.
The recipe's written in letters of gold
By a family witch who is terribly old.

The rule of this cake is it has to be made
In a wheelbarrow (stirred with a shovel or spade)
At Christmas, the season of love and good will.
Other times of the year it might make you feel ill.

You must nail it together or stick it with glue,
Then hammer it flat with the heel of your shoe.
You must stretch it out thin, you must tie it in knots,
Then get out your paint box and paint it with spots.

What a taste! What a flavour! It's certain to please.
It's rather like ice-cream with pickles and cheese.
In June it would taste like spaghetti and mud,
While its taste in September would curdle your blood.

Oh, what a cake! It looks simply delicious.
Now get out the carving knife, get out the dishes!
Be careful! Be careful! This cake might explode,
And blow up the kitchen and part of the road.

Oh dear! It's exploded! I thought that it might.
It's not very often we get it just right.
Let's comfort the baby, revive Uncle Dan,
And we'll start it all over as soon as we can.

For Christmas – that gypsy day – comes and it goes
Far sooner than ever we dare to suppose.
Once more in December we'll gather to make
That truly remarkable once-a-year cake.

MARGARET MAHY

Nightmare

I never say his name aloud
and don't tell anybody
I always close all the drawers
and look behind the door before I go to bed
I cross my toes and count to eight
and turn the pillow over three times
Still he comes sometimes
one two three
like a shot
glaring at me with his eyes,
grating with his nails
and sneering his big sneer –
the Scratch Man

Oh-oh, now I said his name!
Mama, I can't sleep!

SIV WIDERBERG

151

In the Summer
When I Go to Bed

IN the summer when I go to bed
The sun still streaming overhead
My bed becomes so small and hot
With sheets and pillow in a knot,
And then I lie and try to see
The things I'd really like to be.

I think I'd be a glossy cat
A little plump, but not too fat.
I'd never touch a bird or mouse
I'm much too busy round the house.

And then a fierce and hungry hound
The king of dogs for miles around;
I'd chase the postman just for fun
To see how quickly he could run.

Perhaps I'd be a crocodile
Within the marshes of the Nile
And paddle in the river-bed
With dripping mud-caps on my head.

Or maybe next a mountain goat
With shaggy whiskers at my throat,
Leaping streams and jumping rocks
In stripey pink and purple socks.

Or else I'd be a polar bear
And on an iceberg make my lair;
I'd keep a shop in Baffin Sound
To sell icebergs by the pound.

I think I'd be a chimpanzee
With musical ability,
I'd play a silver clarinet
Or form a Monkey String Quartet.

And then a snake with scales of gold
Guarding hoards of wealth untold,
No thief would dare to steal a pin –
But friends of mine I would let in.

But then before I really know
Just what I'd be or where I'd go
My bed becomes so wide and deep
And all my thoughts are fast asleep.

after THOMAS HOOD

Bedtime

WHEN I go upstairs to bed,
I usually give a loud cough.
This is to scare The Monster off.

When I come to my room,
I usually slam the door right back.
This is to squash The Man in Black
Who sometimes hides there.

Nor do I walk to the bed,
But usually run and jump instead.
This is to stop The Hand –
Which is under there all right –
From grabbing my ankles.

ALLAN AHLBERG

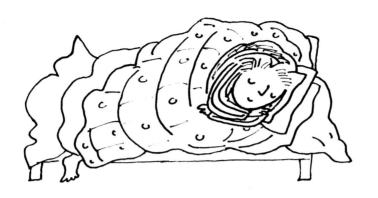

Tough Guy

I'M the big sleeper
rolled up in his sheets
at the break of day

I'm a big sleeper living soft
in a hard kind of way

the light through the curtain
can't wake me
I'm under the blankets
you can't shake me
the pillow rustler

and blanket gambler
a mean tough eiderdown man

I keep my head
I stay in bed

MICHAEL ROSEN

Windy Nights

Whenever the moon and stars are set,
Whenever the wind is high,
All night long in the dark and wet,
    A man goes riding by.
Late in the night when the fires are out,
Why does he gallop and gallop about?

Whenever the trees are crying aloud,
    And ships are tossed at sea,
By, on the highway, low and loud,
    By at the gallop goes he.
By at the gallop he goes, and then
By he comes back at the gallop again.

ROBERT LOUIS STEVENSON

The Horseman

I heard a horseman
Ride over the hill;
The moon shone clear,
The night was still;
His helm was silver,
And pale was he,
And the horse he rode
Was of ivory.

WALTER DE LA MARE

The Falling Star

I saw a star slide down the sky,
Blinding the north as it went by,
Too lovely to be bought or sold,
Too burning and too quick to hold,
Good only to make wishes on
And then forever to be gone.

SARA TEASDALE

The Night
Will Never Stay

THE night will never stay,
The night will still go by,
Though with a million stars
You pin it to the sky;
Though you bind it with the blowing wind
And buckle it with the moon,
The night will slip away
Like sorrow or a tune.

ELEANOR FARJEON

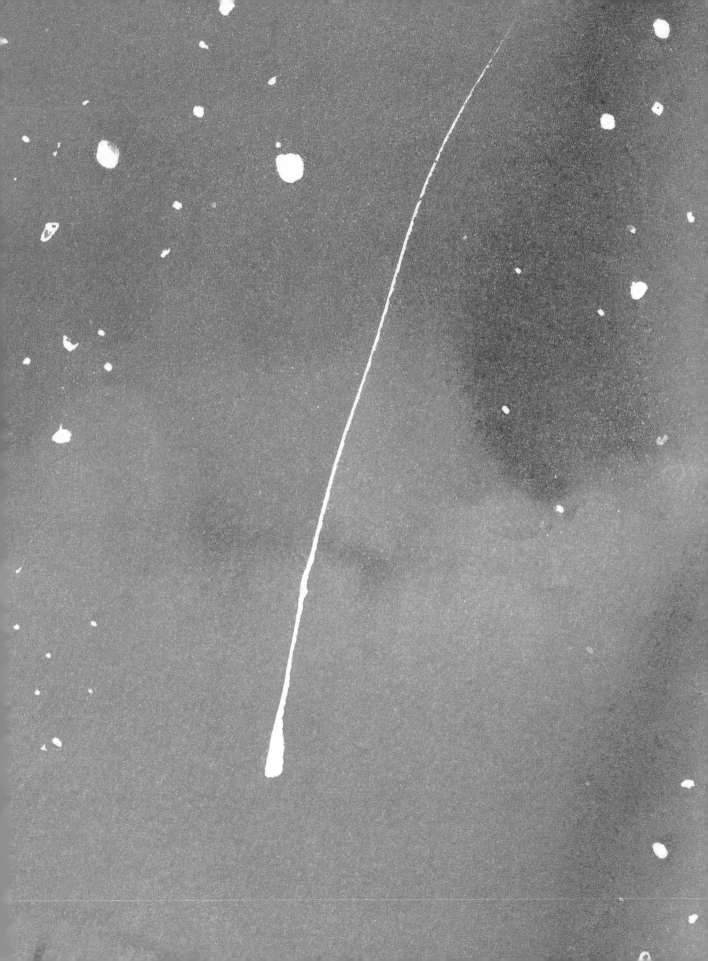

PART THREE
Poems for Older Children

Sky in the Pie!

WAITER, there's a sky in my pie
Remove it at once if you please
You can keep your incredible sunsets
I ordered mincemeat and cheese

I can't stand nightingales singing
Or clouds all burnished with gold
The whispering breeze is disturbing the peas
And making my chips go all cold

I don't care if the chef is an artist
Whose canvases hang in the Tate
I want two veg. and puff pastry
Not the Universe heaped on my plate

OK I'll try just a spoonful
I suppose I've got nothing to lose
Mm…the colours quite tickle the palette
With a blend of delicate hues

The sun has a custardy flavour
And the clouds are as light as air
And the wind a chewier texture
(With a hint of cinnamon there?)

This sky is simply delicious
Why haven't I tried it before?
I can chew my way through to Eternity
And still have room left for more

Having acquired a taste for the Cosmos
I'll polish this sunset off soon
I can't wait to tuck into the night sky
Waiter! Please bring me the Moon!

ROGER McGOUGH

162

I'd Like to Squeeze

I'd like to squeeze this round world into a new shape

I'd like to squeeze this round world

like a tube of toothpaste

I'd like to squeeze this round world
fair and square

I'd like to squeeze it and squeeze it

till everybody had an equal share

JOHN AGARD

Our Baby

WE'VE got a new baby
at our house

they call her Mandy Jane

she's fat and bald
with a line in charm
that's an absolute pain
when you've seen it all before

there's six of us now

so this new one's
got a lot of stick to come

but I reckon if anybody else
gets at her
he'd best know how to run

because
well

she's our kid sister
isn't she?

JOAN POULSON

164

My Baby Brother

MY baby brother is a killer
He pulls my hair and throws me down
on the floor and spits in my face and
squeezes my nose and takes off my
glasses and then tries them on and
throws them away and he jumps on
my stomach and he bites my toes and
he counts my fingers and my mother
says, "Ian get off the floor."

IAN AITKEN

Zeroing In

THE tree down the street
has little green apples
  that never get bigger
    never turn red.
They just drop on the ground
  get worm holes
    brown spots.
They're
  just right for stepping on
    like walking on bumpy marbles,
      or green eggs that break with a snap
        just right for gathering
          in a heap behind the hedge
            waiting
              for a target.
Here comes my brother.

DIANE DAWBER

I Hate

I hate the way my mum calls me "Wend".
I've got nothing to do!
I've played all my games and read all my books –
What can I do?

I hate my dad when he's buried in the paper.
"What can I do Dad?"
It's raining and it's cold, I can't go out –
What can I do?

I hate all these fish, when they gulp
Through the glass.
I've nothing to do!
All I can think of is to make faces back
– That's what I'll do.

WENDY SNAPE

Floating a Plate

I like doing the washing up,
squirting green liquid
into the bottom of our red bowl;
watching it sud and foam
like cream soda,
feeling the froth,
as I launch saucers as submarines
cups and pans as diving bells,
in a sea where knives are sharks
and forks become spiny sea-urchins,
while dunked glasses
surface as smiling and hopeful jellyfish
that slip through the wrinkle and pucker of my fingers.
Most of all though I like washing plates
so I keep them back until last of all.
When the bubbles have all gone and grease floats
on the surface like an oil slick,
carefully I float the plates across a Sargasso Sea
of spaghetti strands and soggy lettuce leaves,
watching as they slowly sink one after the other
like so many pale moons beneath the water;
when the last one has gone
washing up ceases to be fun.

FRANK FLYNN

The Car Trip

MUM says:
"Right, you two,
this is a very long car journey.
I want you two to be good.
I'm driving and I can't drive properly
if you two are going mad in the back.
Do you understand?"

So we say,
"OK, Mum, OK. Don't worry,"
and off we go.

And we start The Moaning:
Can I have a drink?
I want some crisps.
Can I open my window?
He's got my book.
Get off me.
Ow, that's my ear!

And Mum tries to be exciting:
"Look out the window
there's a lamp post."

And we go on with The Moaning:
Can I have a sweet?
He's sitting on me.
Are we nearly there?
Don't scratch.
You never tell him off.
Now he's biting his nails.
I want a drink. I want a drink.

And Mum tries to be exciting again:
"Look out the window
there's a tree."

And we go on:
My hands are sticky.
He's playing with the doorhandle now.
I feel sick.
Your nose is all runny.
Don't pull my hair.

He's punching me, Mum,
That's really dangerous, you know.
Mum, he's spitting.

And Mum says:
"Right, I'm stopping the car.
I AM STOPPING THE CAR."

She stops the car.

"Now, if you two don't stop it
I'm going to put you out the car
and leave you by the side of the road."

He started it.
I didn't. He started it.

"I don't care who started it
I can't drive properly
if you two go mad in the back.
Do you understand?"

And we say:
OK, Mum, OK, don't worry.

Can I have a drink?

MICHAEL ROSEN

Horrible Things

"WHAT'S the horriblest thing you've seen?"
Said Nell to Jean.

"Some grey-coloured, trodden-on plasticine;
On a plate, a left-over cold baked bean;
A cloak-room ticket numbered thirteen;
A slice of meat without any lean;
The smile of a spiteful fairy-tale queen;
A thing in the sea like a brown submarine;
A cheese fur-coated in brilliant green;
A bluebottle perched on a piece of sardine.
What's the horriblest thing *you've* seen?"
Said Jean to Nell.

"Your face, as you tell
Of all the horriblest things you've seen."

ROY FULLER

On Tomato Ketchup

IF you do not shake the bottle,
None'll come, and then a lot'll.

An Accident

AN accident happened to my brother Jim
When somebody threw a tomato at him –
Tomatoes are juicy and don't hurt the skin,
But this one was specially packed in a tin.

Dinner-time Rhyme

CAN you tell me, if you please,
Who it is likes mushy peas?
　　Louise likes peas.
How about Sam?
　　Sam likes spam.
How about Vince?
　　Vince likes mince.
How about Kelly?
　　Kelly likes jelly.
How about Trish?
　　Trish likes fish.
How about Pips?
　　Pips likes chips.
How about Pete?
　　Pete likes meat.
How about Sue?
　　Sue likes stew.
How about Greg
　　Greg likes egg.
How about Pam?
　　Pam likes lamb.

OK, then, tell me, if you can –
How about Katerina Wilhelmina Theodora Dobson?

　　She goes home for dinner…

JUNE CREBBIN

Eddie and the Shreddies

THE other day Eddie
was eating his Shreddies –
you know what Shreddies are:
those little bits of cardboard
you have for breakfast.

Sometimes he forgets where his mouth is
and he stuffs a Shreddie in his ear.
Doesn't worry him
He takes it out and puts it in his mouth.

Anyway,
I left my hairbrush on the table
while he was eating his Shreddies
and I went out of the room.

While I was out
Eddie found somewhere else
to put his Shreddies.
On my hairbrush.

When I came back in
I picked up my hairbrush
and brushed my hair…

Yuk.

Shreddies in my hair.
I looked at Eddie,
Eddie's looking at me.
Big grin on his face.

I knew he had done it.
Last week he put pepper in the raisins.

MICHAEL ROSEN

Blame

GRAHAM, look at Maureen's leg,
She says you tried to tattoo it!
I did, Miss, yes – with my biro,
But Jonathan told me to do it.

Graham, look at Peter's sock,
It's got a burn-hole through it!
It was just an experiment, Miss, with the lens.
Jonathan told me to do it.

Alice's bag is stuck to the floor,
Look, Graham, did you glue it?
Yes, but I never thought it would work,
And Jonathan told me to do it.

Jonathan, what's all this I hear
About you and Graham Prewitt?
Well, Miss, it's really more his fault:
He *tells* me to tell him to do it!

ALLAN AHLBERG

Hullo, Inside

PHYSICAL-education slides
Show us shots of our insides.
Every day I pat my skin,
"Thanks for keeping it all in."

MAX FATCHEN

Homework

HOMEWORK sits on top of Sunday, squashing Sunday flat.
Homework has the smell of Monday, homework's very fat.
Heavy books and piles of paper, answers I don't know.
Sunday evening's almost finished, now I'm going to go
Do my homework in the kitchen. Maybe just a snack,
Then I'll sit right down and start as soon as I run back
For some chocolate sandwich cookies. Then I'll really do
All that homework in a minute. First I'll see what new
Show they've got on television in the living room.
Everybody's laughing there, but misery and gloom
And a full refrigerator are where I am at.
I'll just have another sandwich. Homework's very fat.

RUSSELL HOBAN

Morning Break

ELEVEN o'clock:
seagulls noisy as children
pick up crisps from the empty playground.

ADRIAN HENRI

Boyfriends

CHRISTINE Elkins said to me
under the oak tree
in the Memorial Park –
"I've got 2 $\frac{1}{2}$ boyfriends."
"2 $\frac{1}{2}$?" I said. "2 $\frac{1}{2}$?
How do you work that out?"

"You, Harrybo, Timmy and Rodge,"
she said.
I thought for a moment…
"Me, Harrybo, Timmy and Rodge?
… 4!"
I was just about to say,
"But that makes 4 –"
when suddenly I thought,
"She has halves – HALF boyfriends!…
… 2 halves make one? No. 3 halves plus 1… yes.
But, which ones are the halves?" I thought…
"and who's The One –
THE One?"

I never dared ask her
so I never found out.

MICHAEL ROSEN

Secrets

ANNE told Beth.
And Beth told me.
And I am telling you.
But don't tell Sue –
You know she can't
Keep secrets.

JUDITH VIORST

Shirley Said

WHO wrote "kick me" on my back?
Who put a spider in my mac?
Who's the one who pulls my hair?
Tries to trip me everywhere?
Who runs up to me and strikes me?
That boy there – I think he likes me.

DENNIS DOYLE

Good Girls

G OOD girls
will always go like clockwork
home from school,

through the iron gates
where clambering boys
whisper and pull,

past houses
where curtains twitch
and a fingery witch beckons,

by the graveyard
where stone angels stir,
itching their wings,

past tunnelled woods
where forgotten wolves wait
for prey,

past dens
and caves and darknesses
they go like clockwork;

and when they come
to school again
their homework's done.

IRENE RAWNSLEY

Tall Tales

I saw a silver mermaid with green and purple hair.
I saw her sitting by the river in her underwear.

No you never, you never.

I did.

I saw a rolling calf with twenty-seven toes.
I saw the smoke and fire that was coming from its nose.

No you never, you never.

I did.

I saw the devil dancing reggae in the bright moonlight.
I saw him sting a donkey with his tail the other night.

No you never, you never.

I did.

I saw your father busy looking at your report card.
I saw him searching for you in the house and round the yard.

No you never...you never...you did?

VALERIE BLOOM

179

From Carnival to Cabbages and Rain

THE narrow streets
Are smiles wide
Carnival has come to town.
Granny has a rose in her teeth
The baby wears a crown.
Everyone has come outside
To follow pied piper bands.
Wearing dressing up clothes
Dancing hand in hands.
Hearts and blood
Beat to the drum.
Children free balloons –
"I gave mine to the sun"
A child cries.
Strangers are greeted as friends
Under the blue skies.
The streets vibrate
Deep into the night
And rock from end to ends.
Children sleep on parents' shoulders
Late and light
Weaving Carnival into dreams
Round rainbow bends.

They shop for cabbages today
In narrow streets
Polite and grey.
Glitter shines
Down in the drain
And people say
"Now it can rain."

JULIE HOLDER

Children with Adults

MY auntie gives me a colouring book and crayons.
I begin to colour.
After a while she looks over to see what I have done and says
you've gone over the lines
that's what you've done.
What do you think they're there for, ay?
Some kind of statement is it?
Going to be a rebel are we?
I begin to cry.
My uncle gives me a hanky and some blank paper
do your own designs he says
I begin to colour.
When I have done he looks over and tells me they are all very good.
He is lying,
only some of them are.

JOHN HEGLEY

Pearls

DAD gave me a string of pearls for my birthday.
They aren't real pearls but they look real.
They came nested in deep, deep blue velvet
    in a hinged box with a silvery lid.
His sister had some like them when she was my age.
She was thrilled.
He thought I'd really like them.
I said I did.

I love the box.

JEAN LITTLE

Bees, Bothered by Bold Bears, Behave Badly

"YOUR honey or your life!" says the bold burglar bear,
     As he climbs up the tree where the bees have their lair.
"Burglars! Burglars!" The tree begins to hum.
   "Sharpen up your stings, brothers! Tighten up your
      wings, brothers!
Beat the alarm on the big brass drum!
   Watch yourself, bear, for
         here
            we
               come!"

Then the big black bees buzz out from their lair,
With sharp stings ready zoom down on the bear.
   "Ouch! Ouch! Ouch! Don't be so rough!"
      He slithers down the tree, squalling, "Hey, let me
         be!" Bawling,
   "Keep your old honey. Horrid sticky stuff!
      I'm going home, for
         I've
            had
               enough!"

WALTER R. BROOKS

Spider

I'M told that the spider
Has coiled up inside her
Enough silky material
To spin an aerial
One-way track
To the moon and back;
Whilst I
Cannot even catch a fly.

FRANK COLLYMORE

If You're Out Shooting

If you're out shooting birds just for fun
Here's something to reflect upon:
Would you find it pleasant
To meet a large pheasant
If he was the one with the gun?

NOEL FORD

Please Tell Me

"Please tell me," the chimpanzee said,
"Is it true, what I've recently read?
Surely it cannot be
You're descended from me,
I thought monkeys were all so well bred."

NOEL FORD

Four Little Tigers

FOUR little tigers
Sitting in a tree;
One became a lady's coat –
Now there's only three.

Three little tigers
Neath a sky of blue:
One became a rich man's rug –
Now there's only two.

Two little tigers
Sleeping in the sun:
One a hunter's trophy made –
Now there's only one.

One little tiger
Waiting to be had:
Oops! He got the hunter first –
Aren't you kind of glad?

FRANK JACOBS

To a Squirrel at Kyle-na-no

COME play with me;
Why should you run
Through the shaking tree
As though I'd a gun
To strike you dead?
When all I would do
Is to scratch your head
And let you go.

W. B. YEATS

Allie

ALLIE, call the birds in,
The birds from the sky!
Allie calls, Allie sings,
Down they all fly:
First there came
Two white doves,
Then a sparrow from his nest,
Then a clucking bantam hen,
Then a robin red-breast.

Allie, call the beasts in,
The beasts, every one!
Allie calls, Allie sings,
In they all run:
First there came
Two black lambs,
Then a grunting Berkshire sow,
Then a dog without a tail,
Then a red and white cow.

Allie, call the fish up,
The fish from the stream!
Allie calls, Allie sings,
Up they all swim:
First there came
Two gold fish,
A minnow and a miller's thumb,
Then a school of little trout,
Then the twisting eels come.

Allie, call the children,
Call them from the green!
Allie calls, Allie sings,
Soon they run in:
First there came
Tom and Madge,
Kate and I who'll not forget
How we played by the water's edge
Till the April sun set.

ROBERT GRAVES

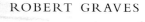

A Small Dragon

I'VE found a small dragon in the woodshed.
Think it must have come from deep inside a forest
because it's damp and green and leaves
are still reflecting in its eyes.

I fed it on many things, tried grass,
the roots of stars, hazelnut and dandelion,
but it stared up at me as if to say, I need
food you can't provide.

It made a nest among the coal,
not unlike a bird's but larger,
it's out of place here
and is quite silent.

If you believed in it I would come
hurrying to your house to let you share my wonder,
but I want instead to see
if you yourself will pass this way.

BRIAN PATTEN

Starfish

WENT star-fishing last night.
Dipped my net in the inky lake
to catch a star for my collection.
All I did was splinter the moon.

JUDITH NICHOLLS

Missing Persons

THE world's most enigmatic smile
  Belongs to Crunch, our crocodile,
Who likes to lie in silent wait
Beside our shrubby garden gate.

And so detectives sometimes come
To question me and Dad and Mum
About the people, big and small,
Who seem to vanish when they call.

But nothing comes of it, of course,
Although we suffer some remorse,
For as they seek a sign or clue
Detectives seem to vanish too.

COLIN THIELE

The Troll

BE wary of the loathsome troll
that slyly lies in wait
to drag you to his dingy hole
and put you on his plate.

His blood is black and boiling hot,
he gurgles ghastly groans.
He'll cook you in his dinner pot,
your skin, your flesh, your bones.

He'll catch your arms and clutch your legs
and grind you to a pulp,
then swallow you like scrambled eggs –
gobble! gobble! gulp!

So watch your steps when next you go
upon a pleasant stroll,
or you might end in the pit below
as supper for the troll.

JACK PRELUTSKY

Macavity: the Mystery Cat

MACAVITY'S a Mystery Cat: he's called the Hidden Paw –
For he's the master criminal who can defy the Law.
He's the bafflement of Scotland Yard, the Flying Squad's despair:
For when they reach the scene of crime – *Macavity's not there!*

Macavity, Macavity, there's no one like Macavity,
He's broken every human law, he breaks the law of gravity.
His powers of levitation would make a fakir stare,
And when you reach the scene of crime – *Macavity's not there!*
You may seek him in the basement, you may look up in the air –
But I tell you once and once again, *Macavity's not there!*

Macavity's a ginger cat, he's very tall and thin;
You would know him if you saw him, for his eyes are sunken in.
His brow is deeply lined with thought, his head is highly domed;
His coat is dusty from neglect, his whiskers are uncombed.
He sways his head from side to side, with movements like a snake;
And when you think he's half asleep, he's always wide awake.

Macavity, Macavity, there's no one like Macavity,
For he's a fiend in feline shape, a monster of depravity.
You may meet him in a by-street, you may see him in the square –
But when a crime's discovered, then *Macavity's not there!*

He's outwardly respectable. (They say he cheats at cards.)
And his footprints are not found in any file of Scotland Yard's.
And when the larder's looted, or the jewel-case is rifled,
Or when the milk is missing, or another Peke's been stifled,
Or the greenhouse glass is broken, and the trellis past repair –
Ay, there's the wonder of the thing! *Macavity's not there!*

And when the Foreign Office find a Treaty's gone astray,
Or the Admiralty lose some plans and drawings by the way,
There may be a scrap of paper in the hall or on the stair –
But it's useless to investigate – *Macavity's not there!*
And when the loss has been disclosed, the Secret Service say:
"It must have been Macavity!" – but he's a mile away.
You'll be sure to find him resting, or a-licking of his thumbs,
Or engaged in doing complicated long division sums.

Macavity, Macavity, there's no one like Macavity,
There never was a cat of such deceitfulness and suavity.
He always has an alibi, and one or two to spare:
At whatever time the deed took place – MACAVITY WASN'T THERE!
And they say that all the Cats whose wicked deeds are widely known
(I might mention Mungojerrie, I might mention Griddlebone)
Are nothing more than agents for the Cat who all the time
Just controls their operations: the Napoleon of Crime!

T. S. ELIOT

My Uncle Paul of Pimlico

MY Uncle Paul of Pimlico
Has seven cats as white as snow,
Who sit at his enormous feet
And watch him, as a special treat,
Play the piano upside-down,
In his delightful dressing gown;
The firelight leaps, the parlour glows,
And, while the music ebbs and flows,
They smile (while purring the refrains),
At little thoughts that cross their brains.

MERVYN PEAKE

The Walrus and the Carpenter

THE sun was shining on the sea,
Shining with all his might:
He did his very best to make
The billows smooth and bright –
And this was odd, because it was
The middle of the night.

The moon was shining sulkily,
Because she thought the sun
Had got no business to be there
After the day was done –
"It's very rude of him," she said,
"To come and spoil the fun!"

The sea was wet as wet could be,
The sands were dry as dry.
You could not see a cloud, because
No cloud was in the sky:
No birds were flying overhead –
There were no birds to fly.

The Walrus and the Carpenter
Were walking close at hand;
They wept like anything to see
Such quantities of sand:
"If this were only cleared away,"
They said, "it *would* be grand!"

"If seven maids with seven mops
Swept it for half a year,
Do you suppose," the Walrus said,
"That they could get it clear?"
"I doubt it," said the Carpenter,
And shed a bitter tear.

"O Oysters, come and walk with us!"
The Walrus did beseech.
"A pleasant walk, a pleasant talk,
Along the briny beach:
We cannot do with more than four,
To give a hand to each."

The eldest Oyster looked at him,
But never a word he said:
The eldest Oyster winked his eye,
And shook his heavy head —
Meaning to say he did not choose
To leave the oyster-bed.

But four young Oysters hurried up,
All eager for the treat:
Their coats were brushed, their faces washed,
Their shoes were clean and neat —
And this was odd, because, you know,
They hadn't any feet.

Four other Oysters followed them,
And yet another four;
And thick and fast they came at last,
And more, and more, and more —
All hopping through the frothy waves,
And scrambling to the shore.

The Walrus and the Carpenter
Walked on a mile or so,
And then they rested on a rock
Conveniently low:
And all the little Oysters stood
And waited in a row.

"The time has come," the Walrus said,
"To talk of many things:
Of shoes – and ships – and sealing-wax –
Of cabbages – and kings –
And why the sea is boiling hot –
And whether pigs have wings."

"But wait a bit," the Oysters cried,
"Before we have our chat;
For some of us are out of breath,
And all of us are fat!"
"No hurry!" said the Carpenter.
They thanked him much for that.

"A loaf of bread," the Walrus said,
"Is what we chiefly need:
Pepper and vinegar besides
Are very good indeed –
Now if you're ready, Oysters dear,
We can begin to feed."

"But not on us!" the Oysters cried,
Turning a little blue.
"After such kindness, that would be
A dismal thing to do!"
"The night is fine," the Walrus said,
"Do you admire the view?

"It was so kind of you to come!
And you are very nice!"
The Carpenter said nothing but
"Cut us another slice:
I wish you were not quite so deaf –
I've had to ask you twice!"

"It seems a shame," the Walrus said,
"To play them such a trick,
After we've brought them out so far,
And made them trot so quick!"
The Carpenter said nothing but
"The butter's spread too thick!"

"I weep for you," the Walrus said:
"I deeply sympathise."
With sobs and tears he sorted out
Those of the largest size,
Holding his pocket-handkerchief
Before his streaming eyes.

"O Oysters," said the Carpenter,
"You've had a pleasant run!
Shall we be trotting home again?"
But answer came there none –
And this was scarcely odd, because
They'd eaten every one.

LEWIS CARROLL

Little Red Riding Hood and the Wolf

As soon as Wolf began to feel
That he would like a decent meal,
He went and knocked on Grandma's door.
When Grandma opened it, she saw
The sharp white teeth, the horrid grin,
And Wolfie said, "May I come in?"
Poor Grandmamma was terrified,
"He's going to eat me up!" she cried.
And she was absolutely right.
He ate her up in one big bite.
But Grandmamma was small and tough,
And Wolfie wailed, "That's not enough!
I haven't yet begun to feel
That I have had a decent meal!"
He ran around the kitchen yelping,
"I've *got* to have a second helping!"
Then added with a frightful leer,
"I'm therefore going to wait right here
Till Little Miss Red Riding Hood
Comes home from walking in the wood."
He quickly put on Grandma's clothes
(Of course he hadn't eaten those).
He dressed himself in coat and hat.
He put on shoes and after that
He even brushed and curled his hair,
Then sat himself in Grandma's chair.
In came the little girl in red.
She stopped. She stared. And then she said,

"What great big ears you have, Grandma."
"All the better to hear you with," the Wolf replied.
"What great big eyes you have, Grandma,"
said Little Red Riding Hood.
"All the better to see you with," the Wolf replied.

He sat there watching her and smiled.
He thought, I'm going to eat this child.
Compared with her old Grandmamma
She's going to taste like caviare.

Then Little Red Riding Hood said, *"But Grandma,*
what a lovely great big furry coat you have on."

"That's wrong!" cried Wolf. "Have you forgot
To tell me what BIG TEETH I've got?
Ah well, no matter what you say,
I'm going to eat you anyway."
The small girl smiles. One eyelid flickers.
She whips a pistol from her knickers.
She aims it at the creature's head
And *bang bang bang*, she shoots him dead.
A few weeks later, in the wood,
I came across Miss Riding Hood.
But what a change! No cloak of red,
No silly hood upon her head.
She said, "Hello, and do please note
My lovely furry WOLFSKIN COAT."

ROALD DAHL

There Was an Old Man with a Beard

THERE was an Old Man with a beard,
  Who said, "It is just as I feared! –
Two Owls and a Hen, four Larks and a Wren,
Have all built their nests in my beard!"

EDWARD LEAR

A Man on a Length of Elastic

A man on a length of elastic
  Decided to do something drastic.
When he jumped off the cliff he
Came back in a jiffy,
And screamed to his friends, "It's fantastic!"

MICHAEL PALIN

A Curious Fellow Called Lamb

A curious fellow called Lamb
  Used to shout things at old tins of Spam
Like, "You silly old tin!"
And, "Where have *you* been?"
Then he'd move on and rubbish the jam.

MICHAEL PALIN

from *The Song of Hiawatha*

By the shores of Gitche Gumee,
By the shining Big-Sea-Water,
Stood the wigwam of Nokomis,
Daughter of the Moon, Nokomis.
Dark behind it rose the forest,
Rose the black and gloomy pine-trees,
Rose the firs with cones upon them;
Bright before it beat the water,
Beat the clear and sunny water,
Beat the shining Big-Sea-Water.
    There the wrinkled old Nokomis
Nursed the little Hiawatha,
Rocked him in his linden cradle,
Bedded soft in moss and rushes,
Safely bound with reindeer sinews;
Stilled his fretful wail by saying,
"Hush! the Naked Bear will hear thee!"
Lulled him into slumber, singing,
"Ewa-yea! my little owlet!
Who is this, that lights the wigwam?
With his great eyes lights the wigwam?
Ewa-yea! my little owlet!"
    Many things Nokomis taught him
Of the stars that shine in heaven;
Showed him Ishkoodah, the comet,
Ishkoodah, with fiery tresses;
Showed the Death-Dance of the spirits,
Warriors with their plumes and war-clubs,
Flaring far away to northward
In the frosty nights of Winter;
Showed the broad white road in heaven,
Pathway of the ghosts, the shadows,
Running straight across the heavens,
Crowded with the ghosts, the shadows.

HENRY WADSWORTH LONGFELLOW

Still the Dark Forest

STILL the dark forest, quiet the deep,
Softly the clock ticks, baby must sleep!
The pole star is shining, bright the Great Bear,
Orion is watching, high up in the air.

Reindeer are coming to drive you away
Over the snow on an ebony sleigh,
Over the mountain and over the sea
You shall go happy and handsome and free.

Over the green grass pastures there
You shall go hunting the beautiful deer,
You shall pick flowers, the white and the blue,
Shepherds shall flute their sweetest for you.

And in the castle tower above,
The princess' cheeks burn red for your love,
You shall be king and queen of the land,
Happy for ever, hand in hand.

W. H. AUDEN

from *Child's Song*

I have a fawn from Aden's land,
On leafy buds and berries nurst;
And you shall feed him from your hand,
Though he may start with fear at first.
And I will lead you where he lies
For shelter in the noontide heat;
And you may touch his sleeping eyes,
And feel his little silv'ry feet.

THOMAS MOORE

Stopping by Woods on a Snowy Evening

Whose woods these are I think I know.
His house is in the village though;
He will not see me stopping here
To watch his woods fill up with snow.

My little horse must think it queer
To stop without a farmhouse near
Between the woods and frozen lake
The darkest evening of the year.

He gives his harness bells a shake
To ask if there is some mistake.
The only other sound's the sweep
Of easy wind and downy flake.

The woods are lovely, dark and deep,
But I have promises to keep,
And miles to go before I sleep,
And miles to go before I sleep.

ROBERT FROST

Night Mail

THIS is the night mail crossing the border,
Bringing the cheque and the postal order,
Letters for the rich, letters for the poor,
The shop at the corner and the girl next door.
Pulling up Beattock, a steady climb –
The gradient's against her, but she's on time.

Past cotton grass and moorland boulder
Shovelling white steam over her shoulder,
Snorting noisily as she passes
Silent miles of wind-bent grasses.

Birds turn their heads as she approaches,
Stare from the bushes at her black-faced coaches.
Sheep-dogs cannot turn her course,
They slumber on with paws across.
In the farm she passes no one wakes,
But a jug in the bedroom gently shakes.

Dawn freshens, the climb is done.
Down towards Glasgow she descends
Towards the steam tugs yelping down the glade of cranes,
Towards the fields of apparatus, the furnaces
Set on the dark plain like gigantic chessmen.
All Scotland waits for her:
In the dark glens, beside the pale-green lochs
Men long for news.

Letters of thanks, letters from banks,
Letters of joy from girl and boy,
Receipted bills and invitations
To inspect new stock or visit relations,
And applications for situations
And timid lovers' declarations
And gossip, gossip from all the nations,
News circumstantial, news financial,
Letters with holiday snaps to enlarge in,
Letters with faces scrawled in the margin,
Letters from uncles, cousins, and aunts,
Letters to Scotland from the South of France,
Letters of condolence to Highlands and Lowlands,
Notes from overseas to Hebrides –

Written on paper of every hue,
The pink, the violet, the white and the blue,
The chatty, the catty, the boring, adoring,
The cold and official and the heart outpouring,
Clever, stupid, short and long,
The typed and printed and the spelt all wrong.

Thousands are still asleep
Dreaming of terrifying monsters,
Or of friendly tea beside the band at Cranston's or Crawford's,
Asleep in working Glasgow, asleep in well-set Edinburgh,
Asleep in granite Aberdeen,
They continue their dreams;
And shall wake soon and long for letters,
And none will hear the postman's knock
Without a quickening of the heart,
For who can hear and feel himself forgotten?

W. H. AUDEN

Green

DUCKLINGS,
Look around.

That's treegreen
filling the sky

and there's grassgreen
running
up the hill
steeply.

The shadowgreen is
pine woods,
dark
old.

The yellowgreen is
young leaf
unfolding,
new
as you.

Breathe green
deeply.

LILIAN MOORE

Ducks' Ditty

ALL along the backwater,
Through the rushes tall,
Ducks are a-dabbling,
Up tails all!

Ducks' tails, drakes' tails,
Yellow feet a-quiver,
Yellow bills all out of sight
Busy in the river!

Slushy green undergrowth
Where the roach swim –
Here we keep our larder,
Cool and full and dim.

Everyone for what he likes!
We like to be
Heads down, tails up,
Dabbling free!

High in the blue above
Swifts whirl and call –
We are down a-dabbling,
Up tails all!

KENNETH GRAHAME

I Asked the Little Boy Who Cannot See

I asked the little boy who cannot see,
  "And what is colour like?"
"Why, green," said he,
"Is like the rustle when the wind blows through
The forest; running water, that is blue;
And red is like a trumpet sound; and pink
Is like the smell of roses; and I think
That purple must be like a thunderstorm;
And yellow is like something soft and warm;
And white is a pleasant stillness when you lie
And dream."

Rainy Nights

I like the town on rainy nights
When everything is wet –
When all the town has magic lights
And streets of shining jet!

When all the rain about the town
Is like a looking-glass,
And all the lights are upside-down
Below me as I pass.

In all the pools are velvet skies,
And down the dazzling street
A fairy city gleams and lies
In beauty at my feet.

IRENE THOMPSON

City Lights

INTO the endless dark
The lights of the buildings shine,
Row upon twinkling row,
Line upon glistening line.
Up and up they mount
Till the tallest seems to be
The topmost taper set
On a towering Christmas tree.

RACHEL FIELD

City

IN the morning the city
Spreads its wings
Making a song
In stone that sings.

In the evening the city
Goes to bed
Hanging lights
About its head.

LANGSTON HUGHES

Flowers Are a Silly Bunch

FLOWERS are a silly bunch
While trees are sort of bossy.
Lakes are shy
The earth is calm
And rivers do seem saucy.
Hills are good
But mountains mean
While weeds all ask for pity.
I guess the country can be nice
But I prefer the city.

ARNOLD SPILKA

Windows

WHEN you look before you go
Outside in the rain or snow,
It looks colder, it looks wetter
Through the window. It is better
When you're outside in it.

When you're out and it's still light
Even though it's almost night
And your mother at the door
Calls you in, there is no more
Daylight in the window
When you're inside looking out.

RUSSELL HOBAN

Fireworks

THEY rise like sudden fiery flowers
That burst upon the night,
Then fall to earth in burning showers
Of crimson, blue, and white.

Like buds too wonderful to name,
Each miracle unfolds,
And Catherine-wheels begin to flame
Like whirling marigolds.

Rockets and Roman candles make
An orchard of the sky,
Whence magic trees their petals shake
Upon each gazing eye.

JAMES REEVES

Flint

AN emerald is as green as grass,
A ruby red as blood;
A sapphire shines as blue as heaven;
A flint lies in the mud.

A diamond is a brilliant stone,
To catch the world's desire;
An opal holds a fiery spark;
But a flint holds fire.

CHRISTINA ROSSETTI

What No Snow?

WHY doesn't it snow?
It's winter, isn't it?
Then it's supposed to snow.
How else can you make snowmen,
Or fight each other with snowballs,
And slide down hills on sledges?

It's not fair, is it?
Soon it will be summer,
Then it'll just rain and rain for months.
Can't anyone tell me,
WHY DOESN'T IT SNOW?

BILL BOYLE

Rain

THERE are holes in the sky
Where the rain gets in,
But they're ever so small
That's why rain is thin.

SPIKE MILLIGAN

Early Spring

DAFFODILS shiver,
huddle away from the wind,
like people waiting at a bus-stop.

ADRIAN HENRI

A Change in the Year

IT is the first mild day of March:
Each minute sweeter than before,
The red-breast sings from the tall larch
That stands beside our door.

There is a blessing in the air,
Which seems a sense of joy to yield
To the bare trees, and mountains bare;
And grass in the green field.

WILLIAM WORDSWORTH

The Shell

IN winter I put a shell to my ear
And through it I hear
The sound of the sea
Answer me.

"Are the donkey and funfair,
Boats and gulls still there?
The pier wading out from the land
And starfish like badges on the sand
Will they be there when I come next year?"
The whispering tide
In the shell replies,
"They will all be here
When you come next year."

STANLEY COOK

Going Barefoot

WITH shoes on,
I can only feel
how hard or soft
the rock or sand is
where I walk
or stand.

Barefoot,
I can feel
how warm mud
moulds my soles –
or how cold
pebbles
knead them
like worn knuckles.

Curling my toes,
I can drop
an anchor
to the sea floor –
hold fast
to the shore
when the tide
tows.

JUDITH THURMAN

Waking Up

Oh! I have just had such a lovely dream!
And then I woke,
And all the dream went out like kettle-steam,
Or chimney-smoke.

My dream was all about – how funny, though!
I've only just
Dreamed it, and now it has begun to blow
Away like dust.

In it I went – no! in my dream I had –
No, that's not it!
I can't remember, oh, it is *too* bad,
My dream a bit.

But I saw something beautiful, I'm sure –
Then someone spoke,
And then I didn't see it any more,
Because I woke.

ELEANOR FARJEON

222

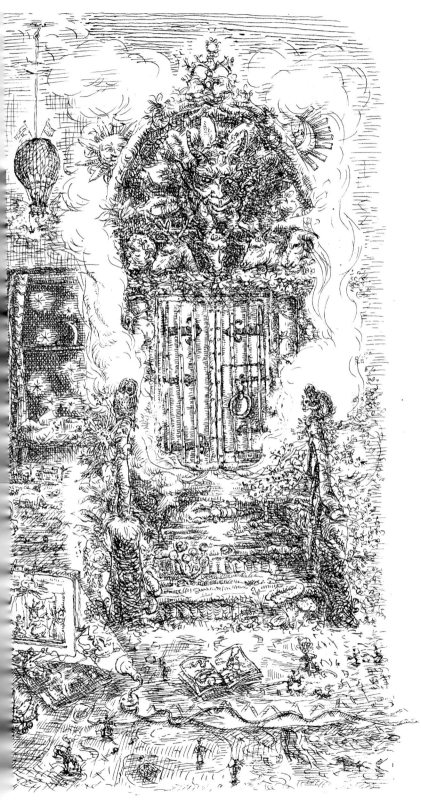

The Door

Go and open the door.
   Maybe outside there's
   a tree, or a wood,
   a garden,
   or a magic city.

Go and open the door.
   Maybe a dog's rummaging.
   Maybe you'll see a face,
or an eye,
or the picture
   of a picture.

Go and open the door.
   If there's a fog
   it will clear.

Go and open the door.
   Even if there's only
   the darkness ticking,
even if there's only
   the hollow wind,
   even if
       nothing
             is there,
   go and open the door.

At least
there'll be
a draught.

MIROSLAV HOLUB

Meet-on-the-Road

"Now, pray, where are you going?" said
                              Meet-on-the-Road.
"To school, sir, to school, sir," said
                              Child-as-it-Stood.

"What have you in your basket, child?" said
                              Meet-on-the-Road.
"My dinner, sir, my dinner, sir," said
                              Child-as-it-Stood.

"What have you for dinner, child?" said
                              Meet-on-the-Road.
"Some pudding, sir, some pudding, sir," said
                              Child-as-it-Stood.

"Oh, then, I pray, give me a share," said
                              Meet-on-the-Road.
"I've little enough for myself, sir," said
                              Child-as-it-Stood.

"What have you got that cloak on for?" said
                              Meet-on-the-Road.
"To keep the wind and cold from me," said
                              Child-as-it-Stood.

"I wish the wind would blow through you," said
                              Meet-on-the-Road.
"Oh, what a wish! What a wish!" said
                              Child-as-it-Stood.

"Pray, what are those bells ringing for?" said
                              Meet-on-the-Road.
"To ring bad spirits home again," said
                              Child-as-it-Stood.

"Oh, then I must be going, child!" said
                                    Meet-on-the-Road.
"So fare you well, so fare you well," said
                                    Child-as-it-Stood.

The Garden Seat

ITS former green is blue and thin,
And its once firm legs sink in and in;
Soon it will break down unaware.
Soon it will break down unaware.

At night when reddest flowers are black
Those who once sat thereon come back;
Quite a row of them sitting there.
Quite a row of them sitting there.

With them the seat does not break down,
Nor winter freeze them, nor floods drown,
For they are as light as upper air,
They are as light as upper air!

THOMAS HARDY

I'm Alone

I'M alone in the evening
when the family sits
reading and sleeping
and I watch the fire in close
to see flame goblins
wriggling out of their caves
for the evening

Later I'm alone
when the bath has gone cold around me
and I have put my foot
beneath the cold tap
where it can dribble
through valleys between my toes
out across the white plain of my foot
and bibble bibble into the sea

I'm alone
when Mum's switched out the light
my head against the pillow
listening to ca thump ca thump
in the middle of my ears.
It's my heart.

MICHAEL ROSEN

Bully Night

Bully night
I do not like
the company you keep
The burglars and the bogeymen
who slink
while others sleep

Bully night
I do not like
the noises that you make
The creaking and the shrieking
that keep me
fast awake.

Bully night
I do not like
the loneliness you bring
the loneliness you bring
The loneliness, the loneliness
the loneliness you bring,
the loneliness you bring
the loneliness, the

ROGER McGOUGH

Shallow Poem

I'VE thought of a poem.
I carry it carefully,
nervously, in my head,
like a saucer of milk;
in case I should spill some lines
before I can put it down.

GERDA MAYER

The Writer of This Poem

THE writer of this poem
Is taller than a tree
As keen as the North wind
As handsome as can be

As bold as a boxing-glove
As sharp as a nib
As strong as scaffolding
As tricky as a fib

As smooth as a lolly-ice
As quick as a lick
As clean as a chemist-shop
As clever as a √

The writer of this poem
Never ceases to amaze
He's one in a million billion
(or so the poem says!)

ROGER McGOUGH

The Poem

IT is only a little twig
With a green bud at the end;
But if you plant it,
And water it,
And set it where the sun will be above it,
It will grow into a tall bush
With many flowers,
And leaves which thrust hither and thither
Sparkling.
From its roots will come freshness,
And beneath it the grass-blades
Will bend and recover themselves,
And clash one upon another
In the blowing wind.

But if you take my twig
And throw it into a closet
With mousetraps and blunted tools,
It will shrivel and waste
And, some day,
When you open the door,
You will think it an old twisted nail,
And sweep it into the dust bin
With other rubbish.

AMY LOWELL

The Female Highwayman

PRISCILLA on one summer's day,
Dressed herself up in men's array;
With a brace of pistols by her side
All for to meet her true love she did ride.

And when she saw her true love there
She boldly bade him for to stand.
"Stand and deliver, kind sir," she said,
"For if you don't I'll shoot you dead."

And when she'd robbed him of all his store,
Said she, "Kind sir, there's one thing more;
The diamond ring I've seen you wear,
Deliver that and your life I'll spare."

"That ring," said he, "my true love gave;
My life I'll lose but that I'll save."
Then, being tender-hearted like a dove,
She rode away from the man she love.

Anon they walked upon the green,
And he spied his watch pinned to her clothes,
Which made her blush, which made her blush
Like a full, blooming rose.

" 'Twas me who robbed you on the plain,
So here's your watch and your gold again.
I did it only for to see
If you would really faithful be.
And now I'm sure that this is true,
I also give my heart to you."

Travel

I should like to rise and go
Where the golden apples grow;
Where below another sky
Parrot islands anchored lie,
And, watched by cockatoos and goats,
Lonely Crusoes building boats;
Where in sunshine reaching out
Eastern cities, miles about,
Are with mosque and minaret
Among sandy gardens set,
And the rich goods from near and far
Hang for sale in the bazaar;
Where the Great Wall round China goes,
And on one side the desert blows,
And with bell and voice and drum,
Cities on the other hum;
Where are forests, hot as fire,
Wide as England, tall as a spire,

Where the knotty crocodile
Lies and blinks in the Nile,
And the red flamingo flies
Hunting fish before his eyes;
Where in jungles, near and far,
Man-devouring tigers are,
Lying close and giving ear
Lest the hunt be drawing near,
Or a comer-by be seen
Swinging in a palanquin;
Where among the desert sands
Some deserted city stands,
All its children, sweep and prince,

Grown to manhood ages since,
Not a foot in street or house,
Not a stir of child or mouse,
And when kindly falls the night,
In all the town no spark of light.
There I'll come when I'm a man
With a camel caravan;
Light a flower in the gloom
Of some dusty dining-room;
See the pictures on the walls,
Heroes, fights, and festivals;
And in a corner find the toys
Of the old Egyptian boys.

ROBERT LOUIS STEVENSON

The Golden Road
to Samarkand

HASSAN

Sweet to ride forth at evening from the wells,
When shadows pass gigantic on the sand,
And softly through the silence beat the bells
Along the Golden Road to Samarkand.

ISHAK

> We travel not for trafficking alone;
> By hotter winds our fiery hearts are fanned:
> For lust of knowing what should not be known
> We take the Golden Road to Samarkand.

MASTER OF THE CARAVAN

> Open the gate, O watchman of the night!

THE WATCHMAN

> Ho, travellers, I open. For what land
> Leave you the dim-moon city of delight?

MERCHANTS (*with a shout*)

> We take the Golden Road to Samarkand!
> (*The Caravan passes through the gate*)

THE WATCHMAN (*consoling the women*)

> What would ye, ladies? It was ever thus.
> Men are unwise and curiously planned.

A WOMAN

> They have their dreams, and do not think of us.

VOICES OF THE CARAVAN (*in the distance singing*)

> We take the Golden Road to Samarkand.

JAMES ELROY FLECKER

Eldorado

GAILY bedight,
A gallant knight
In sunshine and in shadow,
    Had journeyed long,
    Singing a song,
In search of Eldorado.

    But he grew old –
    This knight so bold –
And o'er his heart a shadow
    Fell, as he found
    No spot of ground
That looked like Eldorado.

    And as his strength
    Failed him at length,
He met a pilgrim shadow:
    "Shadow," said he,
    "Where can it be,
    This land of Eldorado?"

    "Over the mountains
    Of the Moon,
Down the valley of Shadow,
    Ride, boldly ride,"
    The shade replied,
"If you seek for Eldorado."

EDGAR ALLAN POE

PART FOUR

Older Poems and Classic Poetry

Lemons and Apples

ONE day I might feel
Mean,
And squinched up inside,
Like a mouth sucking on a
Lemon.

The next day I could
Feel
Whole and happy
And right,
Like an unbitten apple.

MARY NEVILLE

I'm Nobody! Who Are You?

I'M nobody! Who are you?
Are you nobody, too?
Then there's a pair of us – don't tell!
They'd banish us, you know.

How dreary to be somebody!
How public, like a frog,
To tell your name the livelong day
To an admiring bog!

EMILY DICKINSON

Hugger Mugger

I'D sooner be
Jumped and thumped and dumped,

I'd sooner be
Slugged and mugged…than *hugged*…

And clobbered with a slobbering
Kiss by my Auntie Jean:

You know what I mean:

Whenever she comes to stay,
You know you're bound
To get one.
A quick
   short
   peck
   would
   be
   OK
But this is a
Whacking great
Smacking great
Wet one!

KIT WRIGHT

239

I Am Cherry Alive

"I am cherry alive," the little girl sang,
"Each morning I am something new:
I am apple, I am plum, I am just as excited
As the boys who made the Hallowe'en bang:
I am tree, I am cat, I am blossom too:
When I like, if I like, I can be someone new,
Someone very old, a witch in a zoo:
I can be someone else whenever I think who,
And I want to be everything sometimes too:
And the peach has a pit and I know that too,
And I put it in along with everything
To make the grown-ups laugh whenever I sing:
And I sing: *It is true; It is untrue;*
I know, I know, the true is untrue,
The peach has a pit,
The pit has a peach:
And both may be wrong
When I sing my song,
But I don't tell the grown-ups: because it is sad,
And I want them to laugh just like I do
Because they grew up
And forgot what they knew
And they are sure
I will forget it some day too.
They are wrong. They are wrong.
When I sang my song, I knew, I knew!
I am red, I am gold,
I am green, I am blue,
I will always be me,
I will always be new!"

DELMORE SCHWARTZ

maggie and milly and molly and may

maggie and milly and molly and may
went down to the beach (to play one day)

and maggie discovered a shell that sang
so sweetly she couldn't remember her troubles, and

milly befriended a stranded star
whose rays five languid fingers were;

and molly was chased by a horrible thing
which raced sideways while blowing bubbles: and

may came home with a smooth round stone
as small as a world and as large as alone.

For whatever we lose (like a you or a me)
it's always ourselves we find in the sea

E. E. Cummings

Woman Work

I'VE got the children to tend
The clothes to mend
The floor to mop
The food to shop
Then the chicken to fry
The baby to dry
I got company to feed
The garden to weed
I've got shirts to press
The tots to dress
The cane to be cut
I gotta clean up this hut
Then see about the sick
And the cotton to pick.

Shine on me, sunshine
Rain on me, rain
Fall softly, dewdrops
And cool my brow again.

Storm, blow me from here
With your fiercest wind
Let me float across the sky
'Til I can rest again.

Fall gently, snowflakes
Cover me with white
Cold icy kisses and
Let me rest tonight.

Sun, rain, curving sky
Mountain, oceans, leaf and stone
Star shine, moon glow
You're all that I can call my own.

MAYA ANGELOU

Dream Variations

To fling my arms wide
In some place of the sun,
To whirl and to dance
Till the white day is done.
Then rest at cool evening
Beneath a tall tree
While night comes on gently,
    Dark like me –
That is my dream!

To fling my arms wide
In the face of the sun,
Dance! Whirl! Whirl!
Till the quick day is done.
Rest at pale evening…
A tall, slim tree…
Night coming tenderly
    Black like me.

LANGSTON HUGHES

Follower

MY father worked with a horse-plough,
His shoulders globed like a full sail strung
Between the shafts and the furrow.
The horses strained at his clicking tongue.

An expert. He would set the wing
And fit the bright steel-pointed sock.
The sod rolled over without breaking.
At the headrig, with a single pluck

Of reins, the sweating team turned round
And back into the land. His eye
Narrowed and angled at the ground,
Mapping the furrow exactly.

I stumbled in his hob-nailed wake,
Fell sometimes on the polished sod;
Sometimes he rode me on his back
Dipping and rising to his plod.

I wanted to grow up and plough,
To close one eye, stiffen my arm.
All I ever did was follow
In his broad shadow round the farm.

I was a nuisance, tripping, falling,
Yapping always. But today
It is my father who keeps stumbling
Behind me, and will not go away.

SEAMUS HEANEY

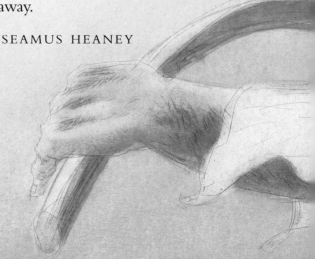

Lost and Found

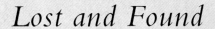

IN my parents' eyes I see
The child that I was meant to be
But who's gone missing? Them or me?

And who is it owns this tangled ground
Where each of us plays lost and found
Until there's nobody around?

JOHN MOLE

Why Is It?

WHY is it,
That,
In our bathroom,
It's not the dirtiest
Or the strongest
Who stays longest?
BUT
It always seems to be
The one who gets there
Just ahead
Of me.

Why is it
That people fret
When they're wet,
With loud cries
And soap in their eyes
And agonised howls,
Because they forget
Their towels?

Why is it that –
When *I'm* in the bath,
Steaming and dreaming,
My toes just showing
And the hot water flowing,
That other people
Yell and say,
"Are you there to stay
Or just on a visit?"

Why is it?

MAX FATCHEN

246

Who'd Be a Juggler?

LAST night, in front of thousands of people,
he placed a pencil on his nose
and balanced a chair upright on it
while he spun a dozen plates behind his back.
Then he slowly stood on his head to read a book
at the same time as he transferred the lot
to the big toe of his left foot.
They said it was impossible.

This morning, in our own kitchen,
I ask him to help with the washing-up –
so he gets up, knocks over a chair,
trips over the cat, swears, drops the tray
and smashes the whole blooming lot!
You wouldn't think it was possible.

CICELY HERBERT

Rodge Said

RODGE said,
"Teachers – they want it all ways –
you're jumping up and down on a chair
or something
and they grab hold of you and say,
'Would you do that sort of thing in your own home?'

"So you say, 'No.'
And they say,
'Well don't do it here then.'

"But if you say, 'Yes, I do it at home,'
they say,
'Well, we don't want that sort of thing
going on here
thank you very much.'

"Teachers – they get you all ways,"
Rodge said.

MICHAEL ROSEN

Private? No!

PUNCTUATION can make a difference.
          Private
     No Swimming
          Allowed

does not mean the same as

          Private?
     No. Swimming
          Allowed.

WILLARD R. ESPY

(Brackets)

IT was Wednesday. Maths. Page 28.
And I was already thinking about tomorrow.
Thursday. Maths. Page 29.

We were doing problems.
The ones where you have to remove the brackets first.

I was on question 13 and right inside a bracket,
When this strange phrase came into my head.
And before I could trap it in a bracket
It shot out of my mouth
Into the classroom.

"Bring on the dancing prunes!"

The room went silent
And thirty pairs of bracket-solving eyes
Swivelled in my direction.
The teacher stopped putting crosses
In somebody's maths book
And looked crossly at me.
"What did you say?"

I could have told him
But instead,
I put a bracket round my reply
And said
"Nothing."

The teacher sighed.
"How would it be if *everybody*
Called out the first thing that came into their heads?"
(Very interesting.)

JOHN COLDWELL

Ten Things to Do with Old Lottery Tickets

MAKE into a small carrier bag
Stick to a pencil and use as a flag
Roll into a tooth-pick
Mop up mouse sick
Make an origami Yeti
Cut to small bits for confetti
Make into a paper aeroplane
Use to cover up an ice-cream stain
Paint gold to decorate the Christmas tree
If it's a winning ticket…give it to me!

ROGER STEVENS

If Only I Had Plenty of Money

IF only I had plenty of money,
I'd buy you some flowers, and I'd buy you some honey,
I'd buy you a boat, and I'd buy you a sail,
I'd buy you a cat with a long bushy tail,
I'd buy you a brooch and a bangle as well,
I'd buy you a church, and I'd buy you the bell,
I'd buy you the earth, I'd buy you the moon −
Oh money, dear money, please come very soon.

PAUL EDMONDS

Waiting for the Call

SITTING in the curtained room
Waiting for the distant call,
Hearing only darkness move
Almost noiseless in the hall
Where the telephone is hunched
Like a little cat whose purr
May be wakened if you press
Ear against its plastic fur,
He sits and knows the urgent noise
Probably will not occur:
There's little hope and, if it does,
He's sure – almost – it won't be her.

VERNON SCANNELL

Don't Quite Know

Why do I feel excited
  When chance decides for us
We are to sit together
In an ordinary school bus?
    Don't quite know.

You pick me for your team (or
More likely I'm the one
Left over for your picking) –
Why is that such great fun?
    Don't quite know.

In the game or on the journey
My bare knee touches yours.
If only for a moment
I see strange opening doors.
    Why that is so
    I don't quite know.

ROY FULLER

252

Mashed Potato / Love Poem

IF I ever had to choose between you
and a third helping of mashed potato,
(whipped lightly with a fork
not whisked,
and a little pool of butter
melting in the middle…)

I think
I'd choose
the mashed potato.

But I'd choose you next.

SIDNEY HODDES

One Perfect Rose

A single flow'r he sent me, since we met.
All tenderly his messenger he chose;
Deep-hearted, pure, with scented dew still wet –
One perfect rose.

I knew the language of the floweret;
"My fragile leaves," it said, "his heart enclose."
Love long has taken for his amulet
One perfect rose.

Why is it no one ever sent me yet
One perfect limousine, do you suppose?
Ah no, it's always just my luck to get
One perfect rose.

DOROTHY PARKER

She Walks in Beauty

SHE walks in beauty, like the night
Of cloudless climes and starry skies;
And all that's best of dark and bright
Meet in her aspect and her eyes:
Thus mellowed to that tender light
Which heaven to gaudy day denies.

GEORGE GORDON, LORD BYRON

A Birthday

MY heart is like a singing bird
Whose heart is in a watered shoot;
My heart is like an apple-tree
Whose boughs are bent with thick-set fruit;
My heart is like a rainbow shell
That paddles in a halcyon sea;
My heart is gladder than all these
Because my love is come to me.

Raise me a dais of silk and down;
Hang it with vair and purple dyes;
Carve it in doves, and pomegranates,
And peacocks with a hundred eyes;
Work it in gold and silver grapes,
In leaves, and silver fleur-de-lys;
Because the birthday of my life
Is come, my love is come to me.

CHRISTINA ROSSETTI

O, My Luve Is Like a Red, Red Rose

O, my luve is like a red, red rose,
That's newly sprung in June:
O, my luve is like the melodie
That's sweetly played in tune.

As fair art thou, my bonnie lass,
So deep in luve am I;
And I will luve thee still, my dear,
Till a' the seas gang dry.

Till a' the seas gang dry, my dear,
And the rocks melt wi' the sun:
And I will luve thee still, my dear,
While the sands o' life shall run.

And fare thee weel, my only luve,
And fare thee weel a while!
And I will come again, my luve,
Tho' it were ten thousand mile!

ROBERT BURNS

from *The Lady of Shalott*

ON either side the river lie
Long fields of barley and of rye,
That clothe the wold and meet the sky;
And through the field the road runs by
    To many-towered Camelot;
And up and down the people go,
Gazing where the lilies blow
Round an island there below,
    The island of Shalott.

Willows whiten, aspens quiver,
Little breezes dusk and shiver
Through the wave that runs for ever
By the island in the river
    Flowing down to Camelot.
Four grey walls, and four grey towers,
Overlook a space of flowers,
And the silent isle imbowers
    The Lady of Shalott.

By the margin, willow-veiled,
Slide the heavy barges trailed
By slow horses; and unhailed
The shallop flitteth silken-sailed
    Skimming down to Camelot;
But who hath seen her wave her hand?
Or at the casement seen her stand?
Or is she known in all the land,
    The Lady of Shalott?

Only reapers, reaping early
In among the bearded barley,
Hear a song that echoes cheerly
From the river winding clearly,
    Down to towered Camelot;
And by the moon the reaper weary,
Piling sheaves in uplands airy,
Listening, whispers, "'Tis the fairy
    Lady of Shalott."

ALFRED, LORD TENNYSON

Ten Tall Oaktrees

TEN tall oaktrees,
Standing in a line,
"Warships," cried King Henry,
Then there were nine.

Nine tall oaktrees,
Growing strong and straight,
"Charcoal," breathed the furnace,
Then there were eight.

Eight tall oaktrees,
Reaching towards heaven,
"Sizzle," spoke the lightning,
Then there were seven.

Seven tall oaktrees,
Branches, leaves and sticks,
"Firewood," smiled the merchant,
Then there were six.

Six tall oaktrees,
Glad to be alive,
"Barrels," boomed the brewery,
Then there were five.

Five tall oaktrees,
Suddenly a roar,
"Gangway," screamed the west wind,
Then there were four.

Four tall oaktrees,
Sighing like the sea,
"Floorboards," beamed the builder,
Then there were three.

Three tall oaktrees,
Groaning as trees do,
"Unsafe," claimed the council,
Then there were two.

Two tall oaktrees,
Spreading in the sun,
"Progress," snarled the by-pass,
Then there was one.

One tall oaktree,
Wishing it could run,
"Nuisance," grumped the farmer,
Then there were none.

No tall oaktrees,
Search the fields in vain:
Only empty skylines
And the cold, grey rain.

RICHARD EDWARDS

Felled Trees

NOBODY has come to burn them,
Long green grass grows up between them,
Up between white boughs that lie
Dead and empty, dry,
That once were full of leaves and sky.

RUTH DALLAS

The Flower-Fed
Buffaloes of the Spring

THE flower-fed buffaloes of the spring
In the days of long ago,
Ranged where the locomotives sing
And the prairie flowers lie low:
The tossing, blooming, perfumed grass
Is swept away by the wheat,
Wheels and wheels and wheels spin by
In the spring that still is sweet.
But the flower-fed buffaloes of the spring
Left us, long ago.
They gore no more, they bellow no more,
They trundle around the hills no more:
With the Blackfeet, lying low,
With the Pawnees, lying low,
Lying low.

VACHEL LINDSAY

Something Told the Wild Geese

SOMETHING told the wild geese
It was time to go,
Though the fields lay golden
Something whispered, "Snow!"
Leaves were green and stirring,
Berries lustre-glossed,
But beneath warm feathers
Something cautioned, "Frost!"

All the sagging orchards
Steamed with amber spice,
But each wild beast stiffened
At remembered ice.
Something told the wild geese
It was time to fly –
Summer sun was on their wings,
Winter in their cry.

RACHEL FIELD

The Tyger

TYGER! Tyger! burning bright
In the forests of the night,
What immortal hand or eye
Could frame thy fearful symmetry?

In what distant deeps or skies
Burnt the fire of thine eyes?
On what wings dare he aspire?
What the hand dare seize the fire?

And what shoulder, and what art,
Could twist the sinews of thy heart?
And, when thy heart began to beat,
What dread hand? and what dread feet?

What the hammer? what the chain?
In what furnace was thy brain?
What the anvil? what dread grasp
Dare its deadly terrors clasp?

When the stars threw down their spears,
And water'd heaven with their tears,
Did he smile his work to see?
Did he who made the Lamb make thee?

Tyger! Tyger! burning bright
In the forests of the night,
What immortal hand or eye,
Dare frame thy fearful symmetry?

WILLIAM BLAKE

Cat Began

Cat began.
She took the howling of the wind,
She took the screeching of the owl
And made her voice.

For her coat
She took the softness of the snow,
She took the yellow of the sand,
She took the shadows of the branches of the trees.

From deep wells
She took the silences of stones,
She took the moving of the water
For her walk.

Then at night
Cat took the glittering of stars,
She took the blackness of the sky
To make her eyes.

Fire and ice
Went in the sharpness of her claws
And for their shape
She took the new moon's slender curve –

And Cat was made.

ANDREW MATTHEWS

The Greater Cats

The greater cats with golden eyes
Stare out between the bars.
Deserts are there, and different skies,
And night with different stars.

VICTORIA SACKVILLE-WEST

The Pig

IN England once there lived a big
And wonderfully clever pig.
To everybody it was plain
That Piggy had a massive brain.
He worked out sums inside his head,
There was no book he hadn't read,
He knew what made an airplane fly,
He knew how engines worked and why.
He knew all this, but in the end
One question drove him round the bend:
He simply couldn't puzzle out
What LIFE was really all about.
What was the reason for his birth?
Why was he placed upon this earth?
His giant brain went round and round.
Alas, no answer could be found,
Till suddenly one wondrous night,
All in a flash, he saw the light.
He jumped up like a ballet dancer
And yelled, "By gum, I've got the answer!

"They want my bacon slice by slice
To sell at a tremendous price!
They want my tender juicy chops
To put in all the butchers' shops!
They want my pork to make a roast
And that's the part'll cost the most!
They want my sausages in strings!
They even want my chitterlings!
The butcher's shop! The carving knife!
That is the reason for my life!"
Such thoughts as these are not designed
To give a pig great peace of mind.

Next morning, in comes Farmer Bland,
A pail of pigswill in his hand,
And Piggy with a mighty roar,
Bashes the farmer to the floor…
Now comes the rather grizzly bit
So let's not make too much of it,
Except that you *must* understand
That Piggy *did eat* Farmer Bland,
He ate him up from head to toe,
Chewing the pieces nice and slow.
It took an hour to reach the feet,
Because there was so much to eat,
And when he'd finished, Pig, of course,
Felt absolutely no remorse.
Slowly he scratched his brainy head
And with a little smile, he said,
"I had a fairly powerful hunch
That he might have me for his lunch.
And so, because I feared the worst,
I thought I'd better eat *him* first."

ROALD DAHL

The Highwayman

PART ONE

THE wind was a torrent of darkness among the gusty trees,
  The moon was a ghostly galleon tossed upon cloudy seas,
The road was a ribbon of moonlight over the purple moor,
And the highwayman came riding –
    Riding – riding –
The highwayman came riding, up to the old inn-door.

He'd a French cocked-hat on his forehead, a bunch of lace at his chin,
A coat of the claret velvet, and breeches of brown doeskin:
They fitted with never a wrinkle; his boots were up to the thigh!
And he rode with a jewelled twinkle,
    His pistol butts a-twinkle,
His rapier hilt a-twinkle, under the jewelled sky.

Over the cobbles he clattered and clashed in the dark inn-yard,
And he tapped with his whip on the shutters, but all was locked and barred:
He whistled a tune to the window; and who should be waiting there
But the landlord's black-eyed daughter,
    Bess, the landlord's daughter,
Plaiting a dark red love-knot into her long black hair.

And dark in the dark old inn-yard a stable-wicket creaked
Where Tim, the ostler, listened; his face was white and peaked,
His eyes were hollows of madness, his hair like mouldy hay;
But he loved the landlord's daughter,
    The landlord's red-lipped daughter:
Dumb as a dog he listened, and he heard the robber say –

"One kiss, my bonny sweetheart, I'm after a prize tonight,
But I shall be back with the yellow gold before the morning light.
Yet if they press me sharply, and harry me through the day,
Then look for me by moonlight,
    Watch for me by moonlight:
I'll come to thee by moonlight, though Hell should bar the way."

He rose upright in the stirrups, he scarce could reach her hand;
But she loosened her hair i' the casement! His face burnt like a brand
As the black cascade of perfume came tumbling over his breast;
And he kissed its waves in the moonlight,
    (Oh, sweet black waves in the moonlight)
Then he tugged at his reins in the moonlight, and galloped away to the West.

PART TWO

He did not come in the dawning; he did not come at noon;
And out of the tawny sunset, before the rise o' the moon,
When the road was a gypsy's ribbon, looping the purple moor,
A red-coat troop came marching –
  Marching – marching –
King George's men came marching, up to the old inn-door.

They said no word to the landlord, they drank his ale instead;
But they gagged his daughter and bound her to the foot of her narrow bed.
Two of them knelt at her casement, with muskets at the side!
There was death at every window;
    And Hell at one dark window;
For Bess could see, through her casement, the road that *he* would ride.

They had tied her up to attention, with many a sniggering jest:
They had bound a musket beside her, with the barrel beneath her breast!
"Now keep good watch!" and they kissed her.
    She heard the dead man say –
Look for me by moonlight;
   Watch for me by moonlight;
I'll come to thee by moonlight, though Hell should bar the way!

She twisted her hands behind her; but all the knots held good!
She writhed her hands till her fingers were wet with sweat or blood!
They stretched and strained in the darkness, and the hours crawled by like years;
Till, now, on the stroke of midnight,
    Cold, on the stroke of midnight,
The tip of one finger touched it! The trigger at least was hers!

The tip of one finger touched it; she strove no more for the rest!
Up, she stood up to attention, with the barrel beneath her breast,
She would not risk their hearing: she would not strive again;
For the road lay bare in the moonlight,
    Blank and bare in the moonlight;
And the blood of her veins in the moonlight throbbed to her Love's refrain.

Tlot-tlot, tlot-tlot! Had they heard it? The horse-hoofs ringing clear –
Tlot-tlot, tlot-tlot, in the distance? Were they deaf that they did not hear?
Down the ribbon of moonlight, over the brow of the hill,
The highwayman came riding,
    Riding, riding!
The red-coats looked to their priming! She stood up straight and still!

Tlot-tlot, in the frosty silence! *Tlot-tlot*, in the echoing night!
Nearer he came and nearer! Her face was like a light!
Her eyes grew wide for a moment; she drew one last deep breath,
Then her finger moved in the moonlight,
    Her musket shattered the moonlight,
Shattered her breast in the moonlight and warned him – with her death.

He turned; he spurred him westward; he did not know who stood
Bowed with her head o'er the musket, drenched with her own red blood!
Not till the dawn he heard it, and slowly blanched to hear
How Bess, the landlord's daughter,
    The landlord's black-eyed daughter,
Had watched for her Love in the moonlight; and died in the darkness there.

Back, he spurred like a madman, shrieking a curse to the sky,
With the white road smoking behind him, and his rapier brandished high!
Blood-red were his spurs i' the golden noon; wine-red was his velvet coat;
When they shot him down on the highway,
    Down like a dog on the highway,
And he lay in his blood on the highway, with the bunch of lace at his throat.

★

And still of a winter's night, they say, when the wind is in the trees,
When the moon is a ghostly galleon tossed upon cloudy seas,
When the road is a ribbon of moonlight over the purple moor,
A highwayman comes riding –
    Riding – riding –
A highwayman comes riding, up to the old inn-door.

Over the cobbles he clatters and clangs in the dark inn-yard;
And he taps with his whip on the shutters, but all is locked and barred:
He whistles a tune to the window, and who should be waiting there
But the landlord's black-eyed daughter,
    Bess, the landlord's daughter,
Plaiting a dark red love-knot into her long black hair.

ALFRED NOYES

Soldiers

IF you're feeling jaded,
Or if you're feeling blue,
Have a little battle…
That's what the soldiers do.

When Genghis Khan was feeling bored
He'd gather up his Golden Horde
And say: "Today we'll devastate
As far as Kiev." And they'd say: "Great!"

A Khan who wants to bring some charm
Into his life will spread some harm.
A little killing, here and there,
Gives life to armies everywhere.

It's very hard, you see, to train
For years in ways of causing pain
Without occasionally trying
Out the latest ways of dying.

The Goths, when life began to pall,
Would simply go and ravage Gaul.
And every Vandal, every Hun,
Agreed on "How To Have Some Fun".

Caesar and Napoleon too
Would all do what good soldiers do,
And – who knows – get a little thrill
From giving chaps the chance to kill.

So if you're feeling jaded,
Or if you're feeling blue,
Have a little battle…
That's what the soldiers do.

TERRY JONES

Soldier Freddy

SOLDIER Freddy
was never ready,
But Soldier Neddy,
unlike Freddy
Was *always* ready
and steady,

That's why,
When Soldier Neddy
Is outside Buckingham Palace on guard in the
pouring wind and rain being steady and ready,
Freddy –
is home in beddy.

SPIKE MILLIGAN

from *The Charge of the Light Brigade*

Half a league, half a league,
Half a league onward,
All in the valley of Death
    Rode the six hundred.
"Forward the Light Brigade!
Charge for the guns!" he said:
Into the valley of Death
    Rode the six hundred.

"Forward the Light Brigade!"
Was there a man dismayed?
Not though the soldier knew
    Someone had blundered:
Theirs not to make reply,
Theirs not to reason why,
Theirs but to do and die:
Into the valley of Death
    Rode the six hundred.

Cannon to right of them,
Cannon to left of them,
Cannon in front of them
    Volleyed and thundered;
Stormed at with shot and shell,
Boldly they rode and well,
Into the jaws of Death
Into the mouth of Hell
    Rode the six hundred.

ALFRED, LORD TENNYSON

Arms and the Boy

L ET the boy try along this bayonet-blade
How cold steel is, and keen with hunger of blood;
Blue with all malice, like a madman's flash;
And thinly drawn with famishing for flesh.

Lend him to stroke these blind, blunt bullet-heads
Which long to nuzzle in the hearts of lads,
Or give him cartridges of fine zinc teeth,
Sharp with the sharpness of grief and death.

For his teeth seem for laughing round an apple.
There lurk no claws behind his fingers supple;
And God will grow no talons at his heels,
Nor antlers through the thickness of his curls.

WILFRED OWEN

Lie in the Dark and Listen

L IE in the dark and listen
It's clear tonight so they're flying high
Hundreds of them, thousands perhaps
Riding the icy, moonlit sky
Men, machinery, bombs and maps
Altimeters and guns and charts
Coffee, sandwiches, fleece-lined boots
Bones and muscles and minds and hearts
English saplings with English roots
Deep in the earth they've left below
Lie in the dark and let them go
Lie in the dark and listen.

Lie in the dark and listen
They're going over in waves and waves
High above villages, hills and streams,
Country churches and little graves
And little citizens' worried dreams
Very soon they'll have reached the sea
And far below them will lie the bays
And coves and sands where they used to be
Taken for summer holidays
Lie in the dark and let them go
Lie in the dark and listen.

Lie in the dark and listen
City magnates and steel contractors
Factory workers and politicians
Soft hysterical little actors
Ballet dancers, reserved musicians
Safe in your warm civilian beds
Count your profits and count your sheep
Life is flying over your heads
Just turn over and try to sleep
Lie in the dark and let them go
Theirs is a world you'll never know
Lie in the dark and listen.

NOËL COWARD

Not a Piece of Cake

THIS is a poem about peace
It's hard to make it work.
Peace is like my poem.
It's not a piece of cake.

LOLA GAMESTER (Aged 13)

If —

IF you can keep your head when all about you
Are losing theirs and blaming it on you;
If you can trust yourself when all men doubt you,
But make allowance for their doubting too;
If you can wait and not be tired by waiting,
Or, being lied about, don't deal in lies,
Or, being hated, don't give way to hating,
And yet don't look too good, nor talk too wise;

If you can dream – and not make dreams your master;
If you can think – and not make thoughts your aim;
If you can meet with triumph and disaster
And treat those two impostors just the same;
If you can bear to hear the truth you've spoken
Twisted by knaves to make a trap for fools,
Or watch the things you gave your life to broken,
And stoop and build 'em up with worn-out tools;

If you can make one heap of all your winnings
And risk it on one turn of pitch–and–toss,
And lose, and start again at your beginnings
And never breathe a word about your loss;
If you can force your heart and nerve and sinew
To serve your turn long after they are gone,
And so hold on when there is nothing in you
Except the Will which says to them: "Hold on";

If you can talk with crowds and keep your virtue,
Or walk with kings – nor lose the common touch;
If neither foes nor loving friends can hurt you;
If all men count with you, but none too much;
If you can fill the unforgiving minute
With sixty seconds' worth of distance run –
Yours is the Earth and everything that's in it,
And – which is more – you'll be a Man, my son!

RUDYARD KIPLING

Not Waving but Drowning

NOBODY heard him, the dead man,
But still he lay moaning:
I was much further out than you thought
And not waving but drowning.

Poor chap, he always loved larking
And now he's dead
It must have been too cold for him his heart gave way,
They said.

Oh, no no no, it was too cold always
(Still the dead one lay moaning)
I was much too far out all my life
And not waving but drowning.

STEVIE SMITH

Advice to Children

CATERPILLARS living on lettuce
Are the colour of their host:
Look out, when you're eating a salad,
For the greens that move the most.

Close your mouth tight when you're running
As when washing you shut your eyes,
Then as soap is kept from smarting
So will tonsils be from flies.

If in spite of such precautions
Anything nasty gets within,
Remember it will be thinking:
"Far worse for me than him."

ROY FULLER

About the Teeth of Sharks

THE thing about a shark is – teeth,
One row above, one row beneath.

Now take a close look. Do you find
It has another row behind?

Still closer – here, I'll hold your hat:
Has it a third row behind that?

Now look in and ... Look out! Oh my,
I'll *never* know now! Well, goodbye.

JOHN CIARDI

The Donkey

I had a Donkey, that was all right,
  But he always wanted to fly my Kite;
Every time I let him, the String would bust.
Your Donkey is better behaved, I trust.

THEODORE ROETHKE

The Purple Cow

I never saw a Purple Cow,
  I never hope to see one,
But I can tell you, anyhow,
I'd rather see than be one!

GELLETT BURGESS

The Elephant

WHEN people call this beast to mind,
  They marvel more and more
At such a LITTLE tail behind,
So LARGE a trunk before.

HILAIRE BELLOC

Ozymandias

I met a traveller from an antique land
Who said: Two vast and trunkless legs of stone
Stand in the desert... Near them, on the sand,
Half sunk, a shattered visage lies, whose frown,
And wrinkled lip, and sneer of cold command,
Tell that its sculptor well those passions read
Which yet survive, stamped on these lifeless things,
The hand that mocked them, and the heart that fed:
And on the pedestal these words appear:
"My name is Ozymandias, king of kings:
Look on my works, ye Mighty, and despair!"
Nothing beside remains. Round the decay
Of that colossal wreck, boundless and bare
The lone and level sands stretch far away.

PERCY BYSSHE SHELLEY

The Lake Isle of Innisfree

I will arise and go now, and go to Innisfree,
And a small cabin build there,
    of clay and wattles made:
Nine bean-rows will I have there,
    a hive for the honey-bee,
And live alone in the bee-loud glade.

And I shall have some peace there,
    for peace comes dropping slow,
Dropping from the veils of the morning
    to where the cricket sings:
There midnight's all a glimmer,
    and noon a purple glow,
And evening full of the linnet's wings.

I will arise and go now,
    for always night and day
I hear lake water lapping
    with low sounds by the shore;
While I stand on the roadway,
    or on the pavements grey,
I hear it in the deep heart's core.

W. B. YEATS

Lemon Moon

ON a hot and thirsty summer night,
The moon's a wedge of lemon light
Sitting low among the trees,
Close enough for you to squeeze
And make a moonade, icy-sweet,
To cool your summer-dusty heat.

BEVERLY McLOUGHLAND

Weeping Willow in My Garden

MY willow's like a frozen hill
Of green waves, when the wind is still;
But when it blows, the waves unfreeze
And make a waterfall of leaves.

IAN SERRAILLIER

The Way Through the Woods

THEY shut the road through the woods
    Seventy years ago.
Weather and rain have undone it again,
And now you would never know
There was once a road through the woods
Before they planted the trees.
It is under the coppice and heath,
And the thin anemones.
Only the keeper sees
That, where the ring-dove broods,
And the badgers roll at ease,
There was once a road through the woods.

Yet, if you enter the woods
Of a summer evening late,
When the night-air cools on the trout-ringed pools
Where the otter whistles his mate,
(They fear not men in the woods,
Because they see so few),
You will hear the beat of a horse's feet,
And the swish of a skirt in the dew,
Steadily cantering through
The misty solitudes
As though they perfectly knew
The old lost road through the woods…
But there is no road through the woods!

RUDYARD KIPLING

Evening: Ponte al Mare, Pisa

THE sun is set; the swallows are asleep;
  The bats are flitting fast in the grey air;
The slow soft toads out of damp corners creep,
And evening's breath, wandering here and there
Over the quivering surface of the stream,
Wakes not one ripple from its summer dream.

There is no dew on the dry grass tonight,
Nor damp within the shadow of the trees;
The wind is intermitting, dry, and light;
And in the inconstant motion of the breeze
The dust and straws are driven up and down,
And whirled about the pavement of the town.

Within the surface of the fleeting river
The wrinkled image of the city lay,
Immovably unquiet, and for ever
It trembles, but it never fades away…

PERCY BYSSHE SHELLEY

from *To Autumn*

SEASON of mists and mellow fruitfulness,
Close bosom-friend of the maturing sun,
Conspiring with him how to load and bless
With fruit the vines that round the thatch-eves run;
To bend with apples the mossed cottage-trees,
And fill all fruit with ripeness to the core;
To swell the gourd, and plump the hazel shells
With a sweet kernel; to set budding more,
And still more, later flowers for the bees,
Until they think warm days will never cease,
For Summer has o'er-brimmed their clammy cells.

JOHN KEATS

There Came a Day

THERE came a day that caught the summer
          Wrung its neck
Plucked it
And ate it.

Now what shall I do with the trees?
The day said, the day said.
Strip them bare, strip them bare.
Let's see what is really there.

And what shall I do with the sun?
The day said, the day said.
Roll him away till he's cold and small.
He'll come back rested if he comes back at all.

And what shall I do with the birds?
The day said, the day said.
The birds I've frightened, let them flit,
I'll hang out pork for the brave tomtit.

And what shall I do with the seed?
The day said, the day said.
Bury it deep, see what it's worth.
See if it can stand the earth.

What shall I do with the people?
The day said, the day said.
Stuff them with apple and blackberry pie –
They'll love me then till the day they die.

There came this day and he was autumn.
His mouth was wide
And red as a sunset.
His tail was an icicle.

TED HUGHES

287

Mushrooms

OVERNIGHT, very
Whitely, discreetly,
Very quietly
Our toes, our noses
Take hold on the loam,
Acquire the air.

Nobody sees us,
Stops us, betrays us;
The small grains make room.

Soft fists insist on
Heaving the needles,
The leafy bedding,

Even the paving.
Our hammers, our rams,
Earless and eyeless,

Perfectly voiceless,
Widen the crannies,
Shoulder through holes. We

Diet on water,
On crumbs of shadow,
Bland-mannered, asking

Little or nothing.
So many of us!
So many of us!

We are shelves, we are
Tables, we are meek,
We are edible,

Nudgers and shovers
In spite of ourselves,
Our kind multiplies;

We shall by morning
Inherit the earth.
Our foot's in the door.

SYLVIA PLATH

Pleasant Sounds

THE rustling of leaves under the feet in woods and under hedges;
The crumping of cat-ice and snow down wood-rides, narrow lanes, and
every street causeway;
Rustling through a wood or rather rushing, while the wind halloos in the oak-
top like thunder;
The rustle of birds' wings startled from their nests or flying unseen into
the bushes;
The whizzing of larger birds overhead in a wood, such as crows, puddocks,
buzzards;
The trample of robins and woodlarks on the brown leaves, and the patter of
squirrels on the green moss;
The fall of an acorn on the ground, the pattering of nuts on the hazel branches as
they fall from ripeness;
The flirt of the groundlark's wing from the stubbles – how sweet such pictures on
dewy mornings, when the dew flashes from its brown feathers!

JOHN CLARE

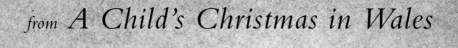

from *A Child's Christmas in Wales*

THERE are always Uncles at Christmas.
The same Uncles. And on Christmas mornings,
with dog-disturbing whistle and sugar fags,
I would scour the swatched town for the news of
the little world, and find always a dead bird
by the white Post Office or by the deserted swings;
perhaps a robin, all but one of his fires out.
Men and women wading or scooping back from chapel,
with taproom noses and wind-bussed cheeks,
all albinos, huddled their stiff black jarring
feathers against the irreligious snow.
Mistletoe hung from the gas brackets in all
the front parlours; there was sherry and walnuts
and bottled beer and crackers by the dessertspoons;
and cats in their fur-abouts watched the fires;
and the high-heaped fire spat, all ready for
the chestnuts and the mulling pokers.

DYLAN THOMAS

Starlings

THIS cold grey winter afternoon
The starlings
On the television aerial
Look like sultanas
On a stalk.

LUCY HOSEGOOD

Small, Smaller

I thought that I knew all there was to know
Of being small, until I saw once, black against the snow,
A shrew, trapped in my footprint, jump and fall
And jump again and fall, the hole too deep, the walls too tall.

RUSSELL HOBAN

Thaw

OVER the land freckled with snow half-thawed
The speculating rooks at their nests cawed
And saw from elm-tops, delicate as flower of grass,
What we below could not see, Winter pass.

EDWARD THOMAS

The Daffodils

I wander'd lonely as a cloud
That floats on high o'er vales and hills,
When all at once I saw a crowd,
A host of golden daffodils,
Beside the lake, beneath the trees,
Fluttering and dancing in the breeze.

Continuous as the stars that shine
And twinkle on the milky way,
They stretch'd in never-ending line
Along the margin of a bay:
Ten thousand saw I at a glance
Tossing their heads in sprightly dance.

The waves beside them danced, but they
Out-did the sparkling waves in glee:
A Poet could not but be gay
In such a jocund company!
I gazed – and gazed – but little thought
What wealth the show to me had brought;

For oft, when on my couch I lie
In vacant or in pensive mood,
They flash upon that inward eye
Which is the bliss of solitude;
And then my heart with pleasure fills,
And dances with the daffodils.

WILLIAM WORDSWORTH

Beachcomber

MONDAY I found a boot –
Rust and salt leather.
I gave it back to the sea, to dance in.

Tuesday a spar of timber worth thirty bob.
Next winter
It will be a chair, a coffin, a bed.

Wednesday a half can of Swedish spirits.
I tilted my head.
The shore was cold with mermaids and angels.

Thursday I got nothing, seaweed,
A whale bone,
Wet feet and a loud cough.

Friday I held a seaman's skull,
Sand spilling from it
The way time is told on kirkyard stones.

Saturday a barrel of sodden oranges.
A Spanish ship
Was wrecked last month at The Kame.

Sunday for fear of the elders,
I sit on my bum.
What's heaven? A sea chest with a thousand
    gold coins.

GEORGE MACKAY BROWN

Full Fathom Five

F ULL fathom five thy father lies,
Of his bones are coral made;
Those are pearls that were his eyes;
Nothing of him that doth fade,
But doth suffer a sea-change
Into something rich and strange.
Sea-nymphs hourly ring his knell:
  Ding-dong.
Hark! now I hear them – Ding-dong bell.

WILLIAM SHAKESPEARE

(*The Tempest*)

Cargoes

Q UINQUIREME of Nineveh from distant Ophir
Rowing home to haven in sunny Palestine,
With a cargo of ivory,
And apes and peacocks,
Sandalwood, cedarwood, and sweet white wine.

Stately Spanish galleon coming from the Isthmus,
Dipping through the Tropics by the palm-green shores,
With a cargo of diamonds,
Emeralds, amethysts,
Topazes, and cinnamon, and gold moidores.

Dirty British coaster with a salt-caked smoke stack
Butting through the Channel in the mad March days,
With a cargo of Tyne coal,
Road-rail, pig-lead,
Firewood, iron-ware and cheap tin trays.

JOHN MASEFIELD

Fog

THE fog comes
on little cat feet.

It sits looking
over harbour and city
on silent haunches
and then moves on.

CARL SANDBURG

Kubla Khan

IN Xanadu did Kubla Khan
A stately pleasure-dome decree:
Where Alph, the sacred river, ran
Through caverns measureless to man
    Down to a sunless sea.
So twice five miles of fertile ground
With walls and towers were girdled round:
And here were gardens bright with sinuous rills,
Where blossom'd many an incense-bearing tree;
And here were forests ancient as the hills,
Enfolding sunny spots of greenery.

But oh! that deep romantic chasm which slanted
Down the green hill athwart a cedarn cover!
A savage place! as holy and enchanted
As e'er beneath a waning moon was haunted
By woman wailing for her demon-lover!
And from this chasm, with ceaseless turmoil seething,
As if this earth in fast thick pants were breathing,
A mighty fountain momently was forced;
Amid whose swift half-intermittent burst
Huge fragments vaulted like rebounding hail,
Or chaffy grain beneath the thresher's flail:
And 'mid these dancing rocks at once and ever
It flung up momently the sacred river.
Five miles meandering with a mazy motion
Through wood and dale the sacred river ran,
Then reach'd the caverns measureless to man,

And sank in tumult to a lifeless ocean:
And 'mid this tumult Kubla heard from far
Ancestral voices prophesying war!
    The shadow of the dome of pleasure
    Floated midway on the waves;
    Where was heard the mingled measure
    From the fountain and the caves.
It was a miracle of rare device,
A sunny pleasure-dome with caves of ice!

    A damsel with a dulcimer
    In a vision once I saw:
    It was an Abyssinian maid,
    And on her dulcimer she play'd,
    Singing of Mount Abora.
    Could I revive within me,
    Her symphony and song,
To such a deep delight 'twould win me,
That with music loud and long,
I would build that dome in air,
That sunny dome! those caves of ice!
And all who heard should see them there,
And all should cry, Beware! Beware!
His flashing eyes, his floating hair!
Weave a circle round him thrice,
And close your eyes with holy dread,
For he on honey-dew hath fed,
And drunk the milk of Paradise.

SAMUEL TAYLOR COLERIDGE

299

from The Pied Piper of Hamelin

INTO the street the Piper stept,
  Smiling first a little smile,
As if he knew what magic slept
    In his quiet pipe the while;
Then, like a musical adept,
To blow the pipe his lips he wrinkled,
And green and blue his sharp eyes twinkled,
Like a candle-flame where salt is sprinkled;
And ere three shrill notes the pipe uttered,
You heard as if an army muttered;
And the muttering grew to a grumbling;
And the grumbling grew to a mighty rumbling;
And out of the houses the rats came tumbling,

Great rats, small rats, lean rats, brawny rats,
Brown rats, black rats, grey rats, tawny rats,
Grave old plodders, gay young friskers,
    Fathers, mothers, uncles, cousins,
Cocking tails and pricking whiskers,
    Families by tens and dozens,
Brothers, sisters, husbands, wives —
Followed the Piper for their lives.

From street to street he piped advancing,
And step for step they followed dancing,
Until they came to the river Weser,
    Wherein all plunged and perished!
— Save one who, stout as Julius Caesar,
Swam across and lived to carry
    (As he, the manuscript he cherished)
To Rat-land home his commentary:
Which was, "At the first shrill notes of the pipe,
I heard a sound as of scraping tripe,
And putting apples, wondrous ripe,
Into a cider-press's gripe:
And a moving away of pickle-tub-boards,
And a leaving ajar of conserve-cupboards,
And a drawing the corks of train-oil-flasks,
And a breaking the hoops of butter-casks;
And it seemed as if a voice
    (Sweeter far than by harp or by psaltery
Is breathed) called out, 'Oh rats, rejoice!
    The world is grown to one vast drysaltery!
So munch on, crunch on, take your nuncheon,
Breakfast, supper, dinner, luncheon!'
And just as a bulky sugar-puncheon,
All ready staved, like a great sun shone
Glorious scarce an inch before me,
Just as methought it said, 'Come, bore me!'
— I found the Weser rolling o'er me."

ROBERT BROWNING

Journey of the Magi

"A cold coming we had of it,
Just the worst time of the year
For a journey, and such a long journey:
The ways deep and the weather sharp,
The very dead of winter."
And the camels galled, sore-footed, refractory,
Lying down in the melting snow.
There were times we regretted
The summer palaces on slopes, the terraces,
And the silken girls bringing sherbet.
Then the camel men cursing and grumbling
And running away, and wanting their liquor and women,
And the night-fires going out, and the lack of shelters,
And the cities hostile and the towns unfriendly
And the villages dirty and charging high prices:
A hard time we had of it.
At the end we preferred to travel all night,
Sleeping in snatches,
With the voices singing in our ears, saying
That this was all folly.

Then at dawn we came down to a temperate valley,
Wet, below the snow line, smelling of vegetation;
With a running stream and a water-mill beating the darkness,
And three trees on the low sky,
And an old white horse galloped away in the meadow.
Then we came to a tavern with vine-leaves over the lintel,
Six hands at an open door dicing for pieces of silver,
And feet kicking the empty wine-skins.
But there was no information, and so we continued
And arrived at evening, not a moment too soon
Finding the place: it was (you may say) satisfactory.

All this was a long time ago, I remember,
And I would do it again, but set down
This set down
This: were we led all that way for
Birth or Death? There was a Birth, certainly,
We had evidence and no doubt. I had seen birth and death,
But had thought they were different; this Birth was
Hard and bitter agony for us, like Death, our death.
We returned to our places, these Kingdoms,
But no longer at ease here, in the old dispensation,
With an alien people clutching their gods.
I should be glad of another death.

T. S. ELIOT

The Donkey

WHEN fishes flew and forests walked,
    And figs grew upon thorn,
Some moment when the moon was blood
Then surely I was born;

With monstrous head and sickening cry
And ears like errant wings,
The devil's walking parody
On all four-footed things.

The tattered outlaw of the earth,
Of ancient crooked will;
Starve, scourge, deride me: I am dumb,
I keep my secret still.

Fools! For I also had my hour;
One far fierce hour and sweet:
There was a shout about my ears,
And palms before my feet.

G. K. CHESTERTON

Nature

Wᴇ have neither Summer nor Winter,
Neither Autumn nor Spring.

We have instead the days
When gold sun shines on the lush green cane fields
Magnificently.

The days when the rain beats like bullets on the roofs
And there is no sound but the swish of water in the gullies
And trees struggling in the high Jamaica winds.

Also there are the days when the leaves fade from off guango trees
And the reaped cornfields lie bare and fallow in the sun.

But best of all there are the days when the mango and the logwood blossom

When the bushes are full of the sound of bees and the scent of honey,
When the tall grass sways and shivers to the slightest breath of air,

When the buttercups have paved the earth with yellow stars,
And beauty comes suddenly and the rains have gone.

H. D. CARBERRY

Hurricane

UNDER low black clouds
the wind was all
speedy feet, all horns and breath,
all bangs, howls, rattles,
in every hen house,
church hall and school.

Roaring, screaming, returning,
it made forced entry, shoved walls,
made rifts, brought roofs down,
hitting rooms to sticks apart.

It wrung soft banana trees,
broke tough trunks of palms.
It pounded vines of yams,
left fields battered up.

Invisible with such ecstasy
with no intervention of sun or man –
everywhere kept changing branches.

Zinc sheets are kites.
Leaves are panic swarms.
Fowls are fixed with feathers turned.
Goats, dogs, pigs,
all are people together.

Then growling it slunk away
from muddy, mossy trail and boats
in hedges and cows, ratbats, trees,
fish, all dead in the road.

JAMES BERRY

The Seven Ages of Man

ALL the world's a stage,
And all the men and women merely players:
They have their exits and their entrances;
And one man in his time plays many parts,
His acts being seven ages. At first the infant,
Mewling and puking in the nurse's arms.
And then the whining school-boy, with his satchel
And shining morning face, creeping like snail
Unwillingly to school. And then the lover,
Sighing like furnace, with a woeful ballad
Made to his mistress' eyebrow. Then a soldier,
Full of strange oaths, and bearded like the pard,

Jealous in honour, sudden and quick in quarrel,
Seeking the bubble reputation
Even in the cannon's mouth. And then the justice,
In fair round belly with good capon lin'd,
With eyes severe, and beard of formal cut,
Full of wise saws and modern instances;
And so he plays his part. The sixth age shifts
Into the lean and slipper'd pantaloon,
With spectacles on nose and pouch on side,
His youthful hose, well sav'd, a world too wide
For his shrunk shank; and his big manly voice,
Turning again toward childish treble, pipes
And whistles in his sound. Last scene of all,
That ends this strange eventful history,
Is second childishness and mere oblivion,
Sans teeth, sans eyes, sans taste, sans everything.

WILLIAM SHAKESPEARE
(*As You Like It*)

When I Heard the Learn'd Astronomer

WHEN I heard the learn'd astronomer,
    When the proofs, the figures, were ranged
  in columns before me,
When I was shown the charts and diagrams, to add,
    divide, and measure them,
When I sitting heard the astronomer where he lectured
    with much applause in the lecture-room,
How soon unaccountable I became tired and sick,
Till rising and gliding out I wander'd off by myself,
In the mystical moist night-air, and from time to time,
Look'd up in perfect silence at the stars.

WALT WHITMAN

from *Auguries of Innocence*

To see a World in a Grain of Sand
And a Heaven in a Wild Flower,
Hold Infinity in the palm of your hand
And Eternity in an hour.

WILLIAM BLAKE

309

Index of Titles

Index of Poets

Index of Illustrators

Acknowledgements

We are grateful to the following copyright holders for permission to reprint the material in this book. The publishers apologise for the few instances in which we have been unable to make contact with the copyright holders, and we would be grateful if they would contact the publishers.

New illustrations by Nicholas Allan, Angela Barrett, Quentin Blake, Jonny Boatfield, Jane Browne, Peter Campbell, Vanessa Card, Alison Catley, Fangorn, Claire Fletcher, Maggie Glen, Rachel Isadora, Susie Jenkin-Pearce, Satoshi Kitamura, Bert Kitchen, Anthony Lewis, Nick Maland, Peter Melnyczuk, Hilda Offen, Liz Pyle, John Richardson, Tony Ross, Wil Rowlands, Wendy Smith, Charlotte Voake, Peter Weevers, Doffy Weir, Joan Welti, Paul Welti, Cliff Wright copyright the individual artists 1998. New illustrations by Allan Curless copyright The Estate of Allan Curless.

JOHN AGARD: I'd Like to Squeeze from *Get Back Pimple*, Viking, 1996, reprinted by permission of the author, c/o Caroline Sheldon Literary Agency; The Older the Violin the Sweeter the Tune from *Say It Again Granny*, The Bodley Head
ALLAN AHLBERG: Bedtime and Blame from *Please Mrs Butler* by Allan Ahlberg, Kestrel Books, 1983 copyright © Allan Ahlberg 1983
IAN AITKIN: My Baby Brother reprinted by permission of the Canadian Council of Teachers of English Language Arts
DOROTHY ALDIS: Wasps from *Is Anybody Hungry?* by Dorothy Aldis copyright © 1964 by Dorothy Aldis, reprinted by permission of G P Putnam's Sons, a division of Penguin Putnam Inc
WAYNE ANDERSON: illustration from *Paws and Claws*, Hutchinson Children's Books, 1995, reprinted by permission of the illustrator
MAYA ANGELOU: Woman Work from *And Still I Rise* by Maya Angelou © Maya Angelou 1978, reprinted by permission of Virago Press and Random House Inc
W H AUDEN: Night Mail from *W H Auden: Collected Poems* by W H Auden, edited by Edward Mendelson copyright 1939, renewed 1966 by W H Auden; Still the Dark Forest from *The Ascent of F6* by W H Auden and Christopher Isherwood and *W H Auden: Collected Poems*, both reprinted by permission of Faber and Faber and Random House Inc
BARBARA BAKER: A Spike of Green reprinted by permission of the Estate of Barbara Baker
NICOLA BAYLEY: illustrations from *Nicola Bayley's Book of Nursery Rhymes*, Jonathan Cape, 1975
HILAIRE BELLOC: The Elephant reprinted by permission of The Peters Fraser and Dunlop Group Limited on behalf of The Estate of Hilaire Belloc © The Estate of Hilaire Belloc
ROBYN BELTON: illustrations from *I'm Glad the Sky Is Painted Blue*,

selected by Rosalyn Barnett, reprinted by permission of Julia MacRae Books and Mallinson Rendal
JAMES BERRY: Hurricane © James Berry 1988, reprinted by permission of The Peters Fraser and Dunlop Group Limited on behalf of the author
QUENTIN BLAKE: illustrations from *Revolting Rhymes* by Roald Dahl, reprinted by permission of Jonathan Cape and Random House Inc; *Dirty Beasts* by Roald Dahl, reprinted by permission of Jonathan Cape and Farrar, Straus & Giroux; *Quentin Blake's Nursery Rhyme Book*, reprinted by permission of Jonathan Cape; *The Winter Sleepwalker* by Joan Aiken, Jonathan Cape, 1994 and *Elephants Have the Right of Way* by Sylvia Sherry, Jonathan Cape, both reprinted by permission of the illustrator and A P Watt
N M BODECKER: When All The World Is Full of Snow from *Hurry, Hurry, Mary Dear! and Other Nonsense Poems* by N M Bodecker copyright © 1976 N M Bodecker, reprinted by permission of Margaret K McElderry Books, an imprint of Simon & Schuster Children's Publishing Division and J M Dent, the Orion Publishing Group
RAYMOND BRIGGS: illustrations from *The White Land*, Hamish Hamilton, 1963, reprinted by permission of the illustrator
WALTER R BROOKS: Bees, Bothered by Bold Bears, Behave Badly from *The Collected Poems of Freddy the Pig* by Walter R Brooks copyright © 1953 by Walter R Brooks, renewed by Dorothy R Brooks, reprinted by permission of The Overlook Press, Woodstock, N Y
GEORGE MACKAY BROWN: Beachcomber from *Selected Poems by George Mackay Brown* reprinted by permission of John Murray, London
MARGARET WISE BROWN: The Secret Song from *Nibble Nibble* copyright © 1959 by William R Scott, Inc, renewed 1987 by Roberta Brown Rauch, reprinted by permission of HarperCollins Publishers, USA
JANE BROWNE: illustrations from *Starlight, Starbright*, chosen by Anne Harvey, Julia MacRae Books, 1995, reprinted by permission of the illustrator and publisher
JOHN BURNINGHAM: illustrations from *Seasons*, Jonathan Cape, 1969; *Oi! Get Off Our Train*, Jonathan Cape and Alfred A Knopf, Random House Inc, 1989, copyright ©1989 by John Burningham, all reprinted by permission of the publishers and illustrator
G K CHESTERTON: The Donkey reprinted by permission of A P Watt Ltd on behalf of The Royal Literary Fund
MARCHETTE CHUTE: Drinking Fountain and Undersea reprinted by permission of Elizabeth Roach
JOHN CIARDI: About the Teeth of Sharks from *You Read To Me, I'll Read To You* copyright © 1962 by John Ciardi, renewed © 1990, reprinted by permission of HarperCollins Publishers, USA
JOHN COLDWELL: (Brackets) from *The Slack-Jawed Camel* by John

Coldwell, Stride, Exeter, 1992 and Where Do Teachers Go? reprinted by permission of the author

FRANK COLLYMORE: Spider reprinted by permission of Ellice Collymore

WENDY COPE: Haiku reprinted by permission of Wendy Cope

NOEL COWARD: Lie in the Dark and Listen from *Collected Poems by Noel Coward*, Methuen, reprinted by permission of the publisher

JUNE CREBBIN: Dinner-time Rhyme from *The Jungle Sale* by June Crebbin, Viking Kestrel, 1988 copyright © June Crebbin 1988

E E CUMMINGS: maggie and milly and molly and may from *Complete Poems 1904 - 1962* by E E Cummings, edited by George J Firmage © 1991 by the Trustees for the E E Cummings Trust and George James Firmage, reprinted by permission of W W Norton & Co

ROALD DAHL: Little Red Riding Hood and the Wolf from *Revolting Rhymes*, Jonathan Cape, 1982 and Random House Inc © Roald Dahl Nominee Ltd; The Pig from *Revolting Beasts*, Jonathan Cape, 1983 and Farrar, Straus & Giroux © Roald Dahl Nominee Ltd, both reprinted by permission of the publishers and David Higham Associates

DIANE DAWBER: Zeroing In reprinted by permission of Borealis Press, Canada

GINA DOUTHWAITE: Sweet Tooth and Do Not Disturb the Dinosaur from *Picture a Poem*, Hutchinson Children's Books, 1994

PAUL EDMONDS: If Only I Had Plenty of Money from *Songs and Marching Tunes for Children*, Pitman Publishing, reprinted by permission of Financial Times Management

RICHARD EDWARDS: Ten Tall Oaktrees reprinted by permission of the author, c/o John Johnson (Author's Agent) Ltd

T S ELIOT: Journey of the Magi from *Collected Poems 1909 - 1962* by T S Eliot, Faber and Faber and Harcourt Brace & Company, USA copyright 1936 by Harcourt Brace & Company, USA copyright © 1963, 1964 by T S Eliot, reprinted by permission of the publishers; Macavity: the Mystery Cat from *Old Possum's Book of Practical Cats* by T S Eliot copyright 1939 by T S Eliot, renewed 1967 by Esme Valerie Eliot, reprinted by permission of Faber and Faber and Harcourt Brace & Company, USA

WILLARD R ESPY: Private? No! from *Another Almanac of Words at Play* by Willard R Espy copyright © 1980 by Willard R Espy, reprinted by permission of Harold Ober Associates Incorporated

ELEANOR FARJEON: Cats from *The Children's Bells*, Oxford University Press; The Children's Carol, The Night Will Never Stay and Waking Up from *Silver Sand and Snow*, Michael Joseph, all reprinted by permission of David Higham Associates

MAX FATCHEN: Hullo, Inside, My Dog, Who's There? and Why Is It? reprinted by permission of the author, c/o John Johnson (Author's Agent) Ltd

RACHEL FIELD: City Lights and Something Told the Wild Geese from *Poems* by Rachel Field copyright 1934 Macmillan Publishing Company, copyright renewed © 1962 Arthur S Pederson, reprinted by permission of Simon & Schuster Books for Young Readers, an imprint of Simon & Schuster Children's Publishing Division

AILEEN FISHER: Holes of Green and The Spinning Earth reprinted by permission of the author

CLAIRE FLETCHER: illustration reprinted by permission of the illustrator

FRANK FLYNN: Floating a Plate reprinted by permission of the author

NOEL FORD: If You're Out Shooting and Please Tell Me from *Limeroons* by Noel Ford, Puffin 1991 copyright © Noel Ford 1991

JOHN FOSTER: Shoes from *Clothes Poems*, compiled by John Foster, Oxford University Press © 1993 John Foster, reprinted by permission of the author

ROBERT FROST: Stopping by Woods on a Snowy Evening from *The Poetry of Robert Frost*, edited by Edward Connery Latham, Jonathan Cape and Henry Holt copyright The Estate of Robert Frost, reprinted by permission of the publishers

CHARLES FUGE: illustration from *Monstrosities*, Hutchinson Children's Books, 1989

ROY FULLER: Advice to Children, Horrible Things and Don't Quite Know reprinted by permission of John Fuller

ROSE FYLEMAN: Mice and Witch, Witch from *Fifty-One New Nursery Rhymes* by Rose Fyleman copyright 1931, 1932 by Doubleday, a division of Bantam, Doubleday, Dell Publishing Group Inc, reprinted by permission of Doubleday and The Society of Authors as the Literary Representative of the Estate of Rose Fyleman

ALICIA GARCIA DE LYNAM: illustration from *Mammny, Sugar Falling Down* by Trish Cooke, Hutchinson Children's Books, 1989, reprinted by permission of the illustrator

LOLA GAMESTER: Not A Piece of Cake reprinted by permission of the author

KENNETH GRAHAME: Ducks' Ditty from *The Wind in the Willows* by Kenneth Grahame copyright The University Chest, Oxford, reprinted by permission of Curtis Brown, London

LIZ GRAHAM-YOOLL: illustrations from *A Footprint on the Air*, selected by Naomi Lewis, Hutchinson Children's Books, 1983

ROBERT GRAVES: Allie from *Complete Poems* by Robert Graves reprinted by permission of Carcanet Press Limited

SEAMUS HEANEY: Follower from *New Selected Poems 1966 - 1987* by Seamus Heaney reprinted by permission of Faber and Faber

ADRIAN HENRI: Early Spring from *The Phantom Lollipop Lady*, Methuen © Adrian Henri 1986; Morning Break copyright © Adrian Henri 1986, both reprinted by permission of the author, c/o Rogers, Coleridge & White Ltd, London

CICELY HERBERT: Who'd Be a Juggler reprinted by permission of the author

RUSSELL HOBAN: Small, Smaller from *The Pedalling Man*, Heinemann; Windows and Homework from *Egg Thoughts and Other Frances Songs*, Jonathan Cape, all reprinted by permission of David Higham Associates

MARY ANN HOBERMAN: Brother from *Llama Who Had No Pajama* copyright © 1959 by Mary Ann Hoberman, reprinted by permission of Harcourt Brace & Company and the Gina Maccoby Literary Agency

LUCY HOSEGOOD: Starlings from *Those First Affections*, edited by T Rogers, reprinted by permission of Routledge

LANGSTON HUGHES: City and Dream Variations from *The Collected Poems of Langston Hughes*, Vintage and Alfred A Knopf, Inc copyright © 1994 by the Estate of Langston Hughes, reprinted by permission of David Higham Associates and Alfred A Knopf Inc

SHIRLEY HUGHES: text and illustrations for Duck Weather, Girl Friends and Night Flight from *Rhymes for Annie Rose* by Shirley Hughes, Bodley Head and Lothrop, Lee & Shepard Books, a division of William Morrow and Company, Inc copyright © 1995 by Shirley Hughes, reprinted by permission of the publishers

TED HUGHES: There Came A Day from *Season Songs* by Ted Hughes copyright © 1968, 1973, 1975 by Ted Hughes, reprinted by permission of Faber and Faber and Viking Penguin, a division of Penguin Putnam Inc

BARBARA IRESON: Min reprinted by permission of the author

RACHEL ISADORA: illustration from *City Seen from A to Z* by Rachel Isadora reprinted by permission of the illustrator

CHRISTOPHER ISHERWOOD: The Common Cormorant from *Exhumations* copyright the Estate of Christopher Isherwood, reprinted with permission of Curtis Brown Ltd, London on behalf of the Estate of Christopher Isherwood

TERRY JONES: Soldiers from *Curse of the Vampire's Socks* by Terry Jones reprinted by permission of Pavilion Books

RUDYARD KIPLING: If — and The Way Through the Woods

JOAN POULSON: Our Baby reprinted by permission of the author
JACK PRELUTSKY: The Troll from *Nightmares: Poems to Trouble Your Sleep* by Jack Prelutsky copyright © 1976 Jack Prelutsky, reprinted by permission of Greenwillow Books, a division of William Morrow & Company, Inc and A & C Black
ARTHUR RACKHAM: illustrations reprinted by permission of his family
IRENE RAWNSLEY: Good Girls from *Toughie Toffee*, edited by David Orme, Collins 1989, reprinted by permission of HarperCollins Publishers Ltd
JAMES REEVES: Fireworks and The Magic Seeds from *Complete Poems for Children*, Heinemann © James Reeves, reprinted by permission of The Estate of James Reeves
THEODORE ROETHKE: The Donkey from *The Collected Poems of Theodore Roethke* copyright © 1961 by Theodore Roethke, reprinted by permission of Doubleday, a division of Bantam Doubleday Dell Publishing Group, Inc and Faber and Faber
MICHAEL ROSEN: Jim, I'm Alone and Tough Guy from *Mind Your Own Business*, Andre Deutsch Children's Books, an imprint of Scholastic Ltd © Michael Rosen 1974; Boyfriends and Eddie and the Shreddies from *Quick, Let's Get Out of Here*, Andre Deutsch Children's Books © Michael Rosen 1983; The Car Trip from *The Hypnotiser*, Andre Deutsch Children's Books © Michael Rosen 1988; all reprinted by permission of Scholastic Ltd ; Rodge Said from *You Tell Me* by Roger McGough and Michael Rosen, Kestrel Books, 1979 copyright © Michael Rosen 1979; Doin' The Pig, from *Piggy Poems*, The Bodley Head; Newcomers and Going Through the Old Photos reprinted by permission of the author
TONY ROSS: illustrations from *Love Shouts and Whispers* by Vernon Scannell, Hutchinson Children's Books, 1990; *The Bad Child's Book of Beasts* by Hilaire Belloc, Jonathan Cape, 1991
VICTORIA SACKVILLE-WEST: The Greater Cats copyright the Estate of Victoria Sackville-West, reprinted by permission of Curtis Brown, London
CARL SANDBURG: Fog from *Chicago Poems* by Carl Sandburg copyright 1916 by Holt, Rinehart and Winston, renewed 1944 by Carl Sandburg, reprinted by permission of Harcourt Brace and Company
VERNON SCANNELL: Sweet Song reprinted by permission of Vernon Scannell; Waiting for the Call from *Love Shouts and Whispers*, Hutchinson Children's Books, 1990
DELMORE SCHWARTZ: I Am Cherry Alive © Delmore Schwartz by arrangement with Robert Phillips and Wieser & Wieser, Inc, New York
MARTINA SELWAY: illustrations from *Paws and Claws*, Hutchinson Children's Books, 1995, reprinted by permission of the illustrator
IAN SERRAILLIER: The Tickle Rhyme and Weeping Willow in My Garden reprinted by permission of Anne Serraillier
SHEL SILVERSTEIN: Pirate Captain Jim from *Where the Sidewalk Ends* by Shel Silverstein copyright © 1974 by Evil Eye Music, Inc, reprinted by permission of HarperCollins Publishers, USA and the Edite Kroll Literary Agency Inc, Portland, Maine
STEVIE SMITH: Not Waving but Drowning from *The Collected Poems of Stevie Smith*, Penguin 20th Century Classics copyright © 1972 by Stevie Smith, reprinted by permission of James MacGibbon and the New Directions Publishing Corp
WILLIAM JAY SMITH: The Toaster and Seal from *Laughing Time: Collected Nonsense by William Jay Smith* copyright © 1990 by William Jay Smith, reprinted by permission of Farrar, Straus & Giroux Inc
ARNOLD SPILKA: Flowers Are a Silly Bunch from *Once Upon A Horse* by Arnold Spilka © 1966, reprinted by permission of the author
ROGER STEVENS: Ten Things to Do with Old Lottery Tickets reprinted by permission of the author
PAULINE STEWART: Goodbye Granny from *Singing Down the Breadfruit and Other Poems* by Pauline Stewart, The Bodley Head, 1993
SARA TEASDALE: The Falling Star from *Collected Poems of Sara Teasdale* copyright 1930 by Sara Teasdale Filsinger, copyright renewed © 1958 by

Guaranty Trust Co of New York, Exr, reprinted by permission of Simon & Schuster
DYLAN THOMAS: A Child's Christmas in Wales extract copyright © 1954 by New Directions Publishing Corp, reprinted by permission of New Directions Publishing Corp and David Higham Associates
IRENE THOMPSON: Rainy Nights from *Come Follow Me* by Irene Thompson reprinted by permission of HarperCollins Publishers Limited
CHARLES THOMSON: The Sea-Monster's Snack reprinted by permission of the author
JUDITH THURMAN: Going Barefoot from *Flashlight and Other Poems* by Judith Thurman copyright © 1976 Judith Thurman, reprinted by permission of Marian Reiner for the author
JAMES S TIPPETT: The Park from *Crickety Cricket: The Best-Loved Poems of James S Tippett* copyright 1933, copyright renewed © 1973 by Martha K Tippett, reprinted by permission of HarperCollins Publishers, USA and William Heinemann
HAZEL TOWNSON: Flight of Fancy from *Piggy Poems*, The Bodley Head
JUDITH VIORST: Secrets from *If I Were In Charge of the World and Other Worries* by Judith Viorst copyright © 1981 Judith Viorst, reprinted by permission of Atheneum Books for Young Readers, an imprint of Simon & Schuster Children's Publishing Division
PETER WEEVERS: illustrations from *The Pied Piper of Hamelin*, retold by Peter Weevers, Hutchinson Children's Books, 1991; *Paws and Claws*, Hutchinson Children's Books, 1995, both reprinted by permission of the illustrator
COLIN WEST: Wobble-dee-woo from *What Would You Do with a Wobble-dee-woo?*, Hutchinson Children's Books, 1988; text and illustrations for George Washington, Columbus, Elizabeth I and Ivan the Terrible from *It's Funny When You Look at It*, Hutchinson Children's Books, 1984
SIV WIDERBERG: Nightmare from *I'm Like Me* by Siv Widerberg copyright © 1968, 1969, 1970, 1971 by Siv Widerberg, translation copyright © 1973 by Verne Moberg, reprinted by permission of The Feminist Press at the City University of New York
NOLA WOOD: Me from *Big Dipper*, Oxford University Press, Australia, 1989, reprinted by permission of June Epstein, June Factor, Gwendda McKay and Dorothy Rickards
CLIFF WRIGHT: illustration from *When the World Sleeps* by Cliff Wright, Hutchinson Children's Books, 1989, reprinted by permission of the illustrator
KIT WRIGHT: Dad and the Cat and the Tree reprinted by permission of the author; Hugger Mugger from *Hot Dog and Other Poems* by Kit Wright, Kestrel Books, 1981 copyright © Kit Wright 1981
W B YEATS: The Lake Isle of Innisfree and To a Squirrel at Kyle-na-no from *The Collected Works of W B Yeats, Volume 1: The Poems*, revised and edited by Richard J. Finneran copyright © 1983, 1989 by Anne Yeats, reprinted by permission of Scribner, a division of Simon & Schuster and A P Watt Ltd on behalf of W B Yeats

Design: Paul Welti
Project Editor: Madeleine Nicklin
Typesetting: Peter Howard

THE HUTCHINSON TREASURY OF CHILDREN'S POETRY
A HUTCHINSON BOOK 0 09 176748 2

Published in Great Britain by Hutchinson,
an imprint of Random House Children's Books

First published 1998

3 5 7 9 10 8 6 4

RANDOM HOUSE CHILDREN'S BOOKS
61–63 Uxbridge Road, London W5 5SA
A division of The Random House Group Ltd

RANDOM HOUSE AUSTRALIA (PTY) LTD
20 Alfred Street, Milsons Point, Sydney,
New South Wales 2061, Australia

RANDOM HOUSE NEW ZEALAND LTD
18 Poland Road, Glenfield, Auckland 10, New Zealand

RANDOM HOUSE (PTY) LTD
Endulini, 5A Jubilee Road, Parktown 2193, South Africa

THE RANDOM HOUSE GROUP Limited Reg. No. 954009
www.kidsatrandomhouse.co.uk

A CIP catalogue record for this book is available from the British Library.

Printed and bound in Singapore